My Mother's Man

By O'Sharra

Copyright © 2019 O'Sharra
Published by T'Ann Marie Presents, LLC
All rights reserved. No part of this book may be reproduced in any form without written consent of the publisher, except brief quotes used in reviews. This is a work of fiction. Any references or similarities to actual events, real people, living or dead, or to real locals are intended to give the novel a sense of reality. Any similarity in other names, characters, places, and incidents are entirely coincidental

Acknowledgements

For My Great Grandmother, who never let a man get too close and coined the term **"LOVE MAY BE SUCH A THRILL, BUT IT DON'T PAY NO GOT DAMN BILLS"** Rest in Heaven.

For My Grand Mother, who experienced *"Graveyard Love"*, a love so consuming that even death couldn't break its bonds. Who taught her daughters that survival is more important than love!

For My Mother, who experienced great love and not so great love, who taught me love can feel like Heaven and Hurt like Hell. So, choose carefully and don't regret your choice.

For the Daughter I will have, whom I will teach based on my OWN experiences to not love anyone but GOD as unconditionally as you love yourself.

Generations Of women that have loved, lost and passed both heartache and knowledge down to their daughters; who passed it down to their daughters.

O'Sharra

My Mother's Man Playlist

https://m.youtube.com/playlist?list=PLaFGeFLmX_YUZCRqaerxHGyGu8FuQRJE5

Chapter One
Netta

♫ *Well lay back and relax*
While I put away the dishes (put away the dishes)
Then you and me can rock a bell

You can ring my bell, ring my bell
You can ring my bell, ring my bell
You can ring my bell, ring my bell
You can ring my bell, ring my bell ♫

"Play That Shit, Maddie B!" A drunken lady yelled out while clutching her fried pig ear sandwich in her hand. The chili and cheese piled on the sandwich overflowed, running down her bony arm. Her rough, life heavy drugs, and heavy liquor drinking, made her look like she had been on earth for longer than her 24 years. Her thick hair was perfectly parted straight down the middle and she had one afro puff on each side of her head. Her jean overalls were so tight, I didn't see how she could take a deep breath. Maybe it helped that she couldn't have weighed more than 100 pounds soaking wet.

"Nora Jean, if you don't get your pissy ass off my chair that's going to be the last song you hear tonight!" My mother told her while walking up to the lady, who happened to be her best friend, handing her a Marlboro slim. The cigarette's only purpose was to hold her over until, Frito, the neighborhood drug dealer, brought more powder for her nose.

Maybe my disgust showed on my face because my mother then turned to look at me with the pure unadulterated hate, she reserved only for me.

"Netta, what the hell you looking at?! Go get your hollaing ass brat!" She said in reference to my crying son, Wayne.

The brat my mother spoke of, the one she tried to abort by shoving a metal clothes hanger up my pussy, was the best and worst thing that had ever happened to me, but I loved him with every fiber of my being. I knew how to be a mother because I took care of my mother's children while she enjoyed her life and pretended that she didn't have any, but if I could have chosen the way my son was conceived and with whom, I would have chosen differently.

One Year Prior

It was around 10:30pm when my mother received the call for a plate of her famous hog maws, Cole slaw, and some extra seasoned turnip greens with ham. The liquor house was in full swing and there were, a sea of bell bottoms, weed smoke, and Afros in our apartment by day but "Maddie's Juke Joint "by night. Sweaty bodies filled the downstairs living room as they drank, ate, mixed, mingled, laughed and danced to Green Eyed Smokey and The Miracles croon, about a tighter hold.

"Y'all gonna get in so much trouble if y'all don't get back up these stairs with me!" My brother Jean said with his two fingers in his mouth.

Sitting on the stairs watching the grown folks act a fool was me, my younger sister and brother Edith and Eddie, my younger brother Randall, and my baby sister Willa Mae. By the age of 35 my mother had 10 children and the youngest was seven. The only children with the same father, were her sets of fraternal twins.

"Jean, take your scary ass back up the steps!" I told my fraternal twin brother; I was the oldest by 2 minutes.

By the age of 12 I was the cook, housekeeper, cashier, and DJ. I could cook a meal better than women three times my age, clean the house from top to bottom in record time, take the money for the liquor and food we sold, as well as give the correct change. I even took care of my younger siblings, and kept the tunes coming from our old system, all with my eyes closed but thanks to my mother, I couldn't read nor write. Now at 14 years old, I was the single person my mother depended on the most and ironically the person she treated the worse.

My three older siblings John, Pearly Mae and Laverne, bailed a long time ago, even though they didn't have half the responsibilities my mother placed on my young shoulders.

RIIIIIINNNNGGGG. RIIIINNNNNGGGGG.

My mother's phone rang loud over the music, causing the guests to protest about being disturbed.

"NETTA, WHERE YOUR GROWN ASS AT?! GO GET MY DAMN PHONE!" My mother screamed at the top of her lungs using all the energy in her small frame, when it would probably take less time and effort for her to walk a few feet over to the kitchen and pick up the phone herself.

At 5'10, my mother was thin and pretty enough to be a model. Her high yellow shade attracted the attention of men of multiple ethnicities, and for the right price, any man could end up in her bed. She wore her hair in curls that framed her heart shaped face. Her slanted eyes and wide nose were as memorable as her high cheekbones and big bright smile. I could look at her for hours. She couldn't look at me for minutes though. For some reason every time she spoke to me, it was as if she hated every detail about me and I never understood why.

"COMIN, MA!" I said to her while getting up from the herd and running down the stairs. If I took too long, she would hit me with whatever she could get her hands on, so I tried to do everything she asked, as quick as I could.

"CHECK ON THOSE BEANS WHILE YOU IN THERE!" She said while continuing to roll her thin frame in circles seductively on Mason, one of her regular customers I saw tip toe from her room in the wee hours of the morning; more often than not.

"Maddie's!" I answered the phone with attitude while putting my hand on my well-developed hip.

Slightly shorter than my mother, I was reminded that my body looked too mature for my age, so my mother made sure I dressed in clothes that were as unflattering as possible.

I was my mother's spitting image, except for wider hips and a complexion that was several shades darker. My lips were also bigger than hers and I preferred to wear my thick coarse hair in a big Afro, when my mother didn't let me straighten it. I thought that maybe she didn't like me because I was the darkest of all her children. We had come so far from the days of segregation, but the beauty standard was still the same; the lighter you were, the prettier you were. Personally, I knew a few lighter skinned girls that looked like the bottom of my shoe. So, even if most people didn't feel the same, I knew my glowing black skin was beautiful.

"Yeah, I want to order some of them maws, a little slaw with it, some turnips with the ham bone and some whole cake bread." The man replied through the phone.

"Some to drank?" I asked him like my mother instructed me to do with all call-in orders.

"Yeah, 5th of white."

"Ma, do we got some moe GIN?!" I yelled out asking her, before I confirmed the order.

"Yeah, I got some moe from the store, REE!" She said, which was short for retard. I had gotten so used to the insults I didn't even take offense to them anymore.

"Ok, that will be 8 for the plate and 6 for the Gin, so 14. Who is this?" I asked the man on the other end of the phone.

"No problem, sweetness. And this is Cliff Con." He said in his sexy voice. I snickered under my breath. Old men tried so hard; it was hilarious to me.

"Is this sweet Netta?" He asked laying it on thicker than necessary. Something else I was used to, flirting and sweet talk from old ass men.

"Yessir." I said saying the two words together as if they were one, rolling my eyes upward. This man was working my nerves. My mother told me I didn't have nerves, but I knew deep down inside that I had them and this man, was doing the Mashed Potato all over them.

"Good, now tell Maddie I can't come and get the stuff cause my gout done flared up, got me over here in bed swollen up." He said.

"So, I need you to drop by? MA MR. CLIFF CON SAID HE NEED ME TO DO A DROP OFF, HIS GOUT FLARED UP!" I yelled across the room to my ma, as Mayday ran his gold, ringed fingers all over her thin body, whispering in her ear. Her slim curvy body didn't look like it bared 10 children, I would give her that. My mother's thin, neck snapped up instantly as if she had been dashed with cold water.

"Tell Cliff this ain't no damn food delivery house!" She said rolling her neck, walking towards me to grab the phone.

"Now, Cliff" she started when she snatched the phone out of my hand. She then went quiet as she listened to his response that cut her off. Suddenly her once angry face lit up like Christmas Morning and she was smiling from ear to ear.

"Now that's a big tip! You putting your money where your mouth at now, Cliff. You done said a mouthful." She said smiling like a schoolgirl.

"Ima send Netta by with it soon as it's done, so limp your gimp ass down the steps to unlock the door cause she gotta be back quick. I need her to finish cooking, you ain't the only one hungry round here!" She said smiling.

"Tell Ella I said hey when she makes it home from work." She said in reference to the man's wife before she hung up the phone.

"Carry your little fast ass to drop off the food and come right back! Don't be out there talking to your grown ass friends or looking at no boys, with your hot ass!" She said as she walked seductively back to Mason.

So, I guess that was settled. I hated the way Mr. Cliff Con looked at me, but I knew I couldn't tell ma no. Armed with the carry out plate of food and the paper sack bag for his liquor, I walked down the dark street to his town house. The neighborhood we lived in was always so alive, they nicknamed it the strip. It wasn't hard to find something to get into for you to end up stuck outside all night.

It was a warm night in Georgia and all the girls were dressed half naked. Shorts, tank tops, crop tops, and sandals were everywhere, as I noticed people of all ages standing around. One of the local dealers had his music pumping loudly from his system, as a group of young guys gambled and argued loudly. A young girl I knew from school, walked up to one of the guys in the dice game with a fat, greasy baby on her hip. It was her child and the guy she approached was her baby father. She had been having sex since she was 12 years old because her strung out mother didn't care what she did, when she did it, or who she did it with. My mother was known around Leland Holmes for not playing that shit, so even though my body looked like it was getting worked over, the only thing I was working over was all the soul food I cooked and ate on the daily basis. The food just kept the weight in the right places.

"Hey, Betty!" I spoke to the young girl while she was having the heated argument with the boy about needing pampers for their son.

There was no need for taking the conversation to a private place because in the ghetto, everyone knew everyone's business and slept with everyone's men. They joked that we were all, *one big happy family,* because of the sharing and rotating of partners going on around here. The shit made me sick to my stomach; I vowed when I was ready to start doing the nasty, it would be with a guy as far away from here as I could get.

"Hey, Netta!" She said dismissively switching the fat baby to her other hip and placing the weight on the other side.

"What's up, Netta Boo?!" Her baby's father said to me licking his lips suggestively.

She looked at the boy as if he had grown three heads. I laughed and walked away, throwing my hips a little harder than I had the first time. The dice game paused momentarily as I walked by capturing the attention of the men, some crouched and some standing. I'd secretly changed my clothes from the baggy shirt and stained shorts I wore around the house before I left; I knew I would take the scenic route through the neighborhood. I was sick of being cooped up in my mother's house cooking, cleaning, and taking care of her children, so I would savor this trip.

My plaid grey skirt hugged my hips; the horizontal lines in the skirt were white and the vertical lines were red. I paired it with a black belt cinched tightly around my small waist, to showcase the hourglass I had been blessed with. I wore my mother's hot pink, short sleeved, button down blouse. I loved how tight it was but I wanted it shorter to show my flat stomach, so I tied it into a knot in the front. I knew I looked good; the appreciative glances and side smiles confirmed it.

I knew I wasn't the finest young girl in the hood or even the prettiest, but I learned that it was nothing sexier to men than something they couldn't have. The chase was their biggest aphrodisiac, and I knew that it was my power. I planned to stay a virgin as long as I could, just so they could pant like dogs and imagine what it felt like in between my chocolate, pretty legs. But you know how the saying goes; if you want to make God laugh, tell him your plans.

"Mr. Cliff!" I called out to him as I walked into his overly furnished, dingy apartment.

He lived on the outskirts of our apartment complex and it took me probably 25 minutes to get there, but I had finally made it; drenched in sweat and thankful that he'd left the door opened, because the air was blasting. I had already taken up too much time stopping to chat and walking slow to show my cute outfit, in the areas where the fine boys hung out. If I wanted to slip back in the house without getting caught, I had to get back quickly.

The one-bedroom townhomes in the community were slightly different from the 3 bedroom we lived in. Upon entering the door, the staircase sat immediately to the right. There were so many steps it was no wonder he had a problem with getting down them all.

"Mr. Clifffffff!" I yelled out to him as I took his stairs two at a time, until I came upon his kitchen.

At the top of the stairs there was the entire flat apartment. The round dining room table sat with two chairs directly across from the stove and refrigerator. Further into the apartment was the living room with an old, oriental couch, one throw rug and a million pictures. I never understood why old people felt the need to keep so many pictures.

"Mr. CLI-" I didn't finish my sentence before I turned around and walked squarely into his chest.

"Sorry!" I said backing up a few steps, hoping I didn't hurt his swollen leg and cost my mother her tip.

"Don't worry about it, sugar" He said smiling showing all 5 of the teeth in his mouth.

His shoulders were broad, and he stood at around 6 feet. I would easily give him early 50's, but he was very strong built, due to all of his years of physical labor. His hands were big and calloused, and his low hair cut was so grey it almost looked white. The scariest part about him was his eyes. I'd seen dark pupils before, but I'd never saw black eyes until I looked, into his.

"Well, I'm going to head out." I told him. "Can you grab the money?" I asked.

"Sure, let me go grab it. It must be really hot out there; you are sweating like crazy!" He said laughing and walking into the room to grab the money.

"I got some ice-cold freezer pops in the deep freezer. Grab you one from the top of the pile, they been in the longest!" He called from the other room.

I walked towards the freezer and opened it up. He only had a few in there but if he offered, I sure would take it. It was a long hot walk back home, and it would save me from begging my mother for 50 cents to buy one from the freezer lady that lived next door to us. I know she made good money off those freezers because all the kids loved them.

After bending to reach for my freezer, I turned around and began to lick it feverishly because it was SOOO good. I wasn't sure what flavor this was, but I was sure I'd never tasted it before. The aftertaste was awful, so I licked more to get rid of the terrible taste. I licked and licked until my licks began to slow down. It felt like everything was starting to slow down and my head felt a little heavy. Something wasn't right.

When he finally made it back to the kitchen I was leaning over the table and my vision was slightly blurred. I struggled to look up at him to find him looking over every part of my body, except my face. His eyes roamed over my breast and down to my stomach, I felt like I was going to be sick.

"Excuse me." I said trying to push past him to get back to the staircase, wobbling slightly. I would just tell my mother he took forever trying to find the money and head home. After she kicked my ass she would come back and get it herself; I was fine with that.

"Wait young gul, you gotta get the money." He said smiling and grabbing my arm.

"My Ma- can come back and grab it from you, I have to get back and finish cooking." I told him stammering, trying to get around him as his grip tightened on my arm.

Lord where was his wife, somebody, or anybody right? My stomach was in knots and I was nervous. I felt like I was about to faint as the seriousness of the situation settled around me. Here I was in some strong old ass man's apartment alone, with a tiny ass skirt on, feeling woozy enough to just topple over at any moment.

"She doesn't have to come all this way when you're right here." He said not letting go of my arm. Instead, he was pulling me in the opposite direction, towards the open door that revealed a bedroom.

At that point I was trying with all my might to go downstairs and out the door, but suddenly I felt extremely tired.

"Mr. Cliff, ima sit right here for a quick second. Can you call my mom and tell her where I am?" I said while sitting in his high back, chair.

That was the last thing I remembered saying before everything went dark.

Chapter Two
Netta

"Wake up, little lady." Mr.Cliff Con said to me, slapping my face lightly. When I opened my eyes, I felt extremely groggy.

"What happened?" I asked him as I wiped my face and stretched. I couldn't believe I had fallen asleep; my mother would kill me.

"You fell asleep, gul." He said while helping me to my feet. I staggered slightly, then I felt a dull ache somewhere I had never ached before. I looked down at myself and my clothes were still intact, but I felt bare under my skirt; I didn't have on any panties.

"Here, Here, you gotta go!" he said crushing two 50-dollar bills into my palms. I knew that he had violated me while I slept because he couldn't even look me in my eyes. My chest felt heavy, I couldn't believe this had happened to me.

I walked out of the door with my head held down, prepared for the beating that I was sure was coming when I made it home. I didn't know how long I was gone, but I was sure my mother was waiting. Even worse I was sure if I told her what happened, she wouldn't believe me.

I cried silently to myself as I walked through the apartment complex, while everyone around me continued to laugh, dance, play, and have fun. When I made it to the house, it was too quiet. That let me know all the guests had gone home, so it had to be extremely late. People didn't leave my mother's house till around 3 in the morning, so I had to have been out longer than I thought. I wondered if my mother came out looking for me or just chalked it up to me somewhere being **grown** doing what she told me not to do, caught up somewhere with some little boy.

I stepped up to the door and turned the knob, it turned with ease. I stepped into the house filled with shame and ready to take a hot bath and get into my twin bed with my little sister.

"So you think you grown, huh?" She said sitting on the couch with Mason sitting next to her.

"Ma, it's not like that something bad happened to me!!!" I told her finally saying the words out loud, crying, hoping she would come to me and console me.

"Ain't shit happened to your grown ass! Is that my got damn shirt?" She asked angrily. "Where the hell did that little ass skirt come from? Where the hell you been, Netta? Look at your hair, look at you! You look like you just got fucked, where is my money?" She asked getting in my face.

"Baby, just calm down and hear her out." Mason said to her smoothly while standing from the couch and walking over to my mother. He began to rub her back softly to console her while looking at me lustfully.

"Naw, she ain't got nothing to say. Where is my money, NETTA?!"

I handed her both 50-dollar bills as the tears flowed down my face freely. This was the answer to the question I asked myself before I stepped inside of the house. She hadn't been looking for me and she probably wouldn't have given a damn if I was floating in the Chattahoochee River somewhere.

"WHAT THE HELL DID I DO TO MAKE YOU HATE ME SO MUCH, MA?!" I asked her, screaming. At this point I didn't care who I woke up or who I disturbed. I was sick of this bitch. If I never saw her face again, it would be too soon.

WHAAACKKK!

She slapped me hard across my face.

"I don't know who the hell you talking to! Done got your first little piece of dick and think you grown but I'm the head bitch in this castle, you hear me?!" She said looking me eye to eye. "You smell like sex. Go wash your funky ass!" She said while smirking.

"And next time get more than a few dollars, because if you going to be grown you going in on these bills around here! The little young boy probably told you he cared about you to get the ass, then sent your dumb ass packing. That's why you standing in my face crying, talking about something bad happened! You will be better off when you learn that LOVE MAY BE SUCH A THRILL BUT IT DON'T PAY NO BILLS! YOU BETTER GET THAT GOT DAMN MONEY! He done sent you home with a wet ass and a broken heart, get the hell out my face!" She said waving her hand dismissively, while walking back to the couch, sitting in her spot on the sofa.

I cried as I soaked in the steaming hot bathtub. The only person that continued to break my heart repeatedly was her. No matter how much I did to prove to her that I was worthy of her love, it was never enough. I vowed to never be the type of mother she was to me.

Present Day

♪ *(Ring my bell, ding-dong- don't)*
You Can ring my bell, ring my bell ♪

"Earth to Netta!" My mother said snapping her almond shaped, red nails a few inches away from my nose.

"The brat, the hollain brat! Take your bloody ass upstairs and get him!"

If she wasn't my mother.

I climbed the stairs two at a time to get to my baby, suddenly he stopped crying. Stepping into the tiny room that I shared with my three younger sisters Lucy, Willa Mae, and Edith, I halted as I realized the reason. Sitting on my bed playing with my now laughing baby boy was, Mayday. He looked as sexy as he always did, with his gold, satin, long sleeved shirt, opened all the way to his belly button. Several gold chains laid against his bronze skin. His fitted shirt showed his amazing lean body because he had it tucked inside of his earth toned slacks. His gold platform shoes completed the look and he looked like a super star. I wished it had been him that did it to me that day to make Wayne and not old Mr. Cliff.

His eyes roamed all over my body and I felt my nipples stick out threw my thin crop top. I was sure he saw them too because my perfect breast, were never hidden behind a bra. He licked his big lips and I felt a tingly sensation below.

"He just wanted a little attention." He said to me while looking me up and down. I felt naked under his stare.

"Thank you Mr. Mason-" I started but he stopped me.

"Mister is for old men. Call me Mayday."

I blushed and looked down. "Ok, Mayday."

He stood up from the bed and kissed my son on the forehead before he put him in my arms.

"He's a beautiful boy, I wish he were mine." He said then winked at me and walked out of the door.

My heart sped up; I was sure I had imagined the entire thing. If It was all a fantasy that was fine because it was a beautiful fantasy. I sat on my bed and smiled as I held my son. I was sure that nothing or no one would be able to wipe that smile off of my face for the rest of the day.

"BABY!" My mother called out to Mayday from downstairs.

"I know that hollain ass baby was disturbing you from your nap!"

I heard his platforms clock as he walked down our stairs.

"It's ok, baby. You just gotta get her and the baby out of this house, you know I need my rest!" He replied.

Chapter Three
Netta

"You forgot to wash my underwear so I can have clean one's for school!" My little sister Lucy said. It was the first day of school and I was up with my younger siblings, getting them prepared. The house was chaotic as I combed Lucy, Willa, and Edith's hair, made sure everyone had washed up, and brushed their teeth. I wanted to make sure they were all cleaned up and had clean clothes, even if they were last year's clothes and shoes. On top of that, I had my now one-year old son crying for juice and my attention. Lord what a life!

"Ya'll keep it DOWN, damn! Me and my man trying to sleep!" My mother hollered from the other room. It was funny to me that she wanted us to keep it down, but she hadn't gotten up to check on her own children or to see them off. Just because a woman could have children, didn't mean that she should. I could never abandon Wayne and treat him the way my mother treated us.

"Just put back on the one's you took off, I cleaned everything else so you will be fine, big head. When you come home you will have some clean ones. Now let me slip on some shoes and grab Wayne, so I can walk y'all to the bus stop." I told her while looking for my slide ins.

∞∞∞

> ♪ When the night has come
> And the land is dark
> And the moon is the only light we'll see
> No, I won't be afraid, no I won't be afraid
> Just as long as you stand, stand by me
>
> So darlin', darlin', stand by me, oh stand by me
> Oh, stand by me, stand by me
>
> If the sky that we look upon
> Should tumble and fall
> Or the mountains should crumble to the sea
> I won't cry, I won't cry, no I won't shed a tear
> Just as long as you stand, stand by me

Later that night, as I took a break from being a slave and enjoyed the sweet melody. I let the song take over me as I placed the wooden spoon on the counter next to the stove. Ben E. King crooned softly as my hips took on a life of their own and I slowly moved to the music. This music didn't deserve rushed movements, soft sensual ones would do.

I let my body do what it wanted, no rules or inhibitions like a newly released dove. I felt as if I were the only person in the room, in the house, or even on the planet. Just me and the music.

"So that's how you made Wayne, huh?" Mason asked me seductively leaning on the refrigerator, startling me out of my trance. He had a bad habit of sneaking up on me.

"I didn't know you could move like that, girl!" He said smiling at me.

"You weren't supposed to know." I replied snidely.

"Why you getting cute with me? I'm not your enemy." Mason said to me walking up slowly.

"I hear all the things you say about me and my son, to my mother." I said to him while turning my back on him, to get back to cooking the food.

He walked up to me until he was standing directly behind me. He stood so close I could feel him breathing on the back of my neck. The hairs on the back of my neck stood up and I felt tingling on my lower back. With him pressed firmly against my back, I could no longer stir the food. It took all I had to control my breathing. Lord I wanted this man.

He pressed his lips gently against my neck and my heart felt as if it would leap out of my chest. His kisses trailed up to my ear, before he whispered, "Sometimes you have to have an ally behind enemy lines."

He then grabbed my butt, placing each cheek in one of his massive hands. Involuntary, I backed up on him and began to move my hips, slowly, until I heard a loud commotion that made me jump out of my skin.

"WHAT HAPPENED TO HIS LEG?!" My mother screamed.

My entire body froze for a few seconds before I took off running in the direction towards her voice. When I made it to my mother, the scene I witnessed made me sad enough to cry, but angry enough to take a life. My son wasn't crying, but there was a large gash on the side of his leg that made my blood boil. She told me that she would look after him and rushed me downstairs to cook for her guests, I should have known that she wouldn't keep her damn word. Instead she handed him off to one of her drunk guests who probably wasn't paying him enough damn attention.

"WHAT THE FUCK HAPPENED?!" I asked not thinking but purely reacting. A mother lion ready to defend her cub, I snatched my son from off the floor and slapped the shit out of the drunk man with all the strength I possessed. Before I could go back at him Mayday had already grabbed the man and proceeded to beat him senselessly.

"BABY, PLEASE DON'T! HE HAD TOO MUCH TO DRINK, BUT HE PROBABLY ONLY TOOK HIS EYES OFF HIM FOR A SECOND!" My mother screamed at Mason even though the drunk man could have gotten her only grandchild killed.

"BEAT HIS ASS MAYDAY!" I screamed holding on to my son tightly.

"YOU SHUT THE HELL UP! YOU JUST WANT MY MAN TO GET IN TROUBLE FOR YOUR NAPPY HEAD ASS CHILD! HE AINT HURT THAT BAD. HE'S A LITTLE BOY, HE WILL BE OK!" She screamed in my face; upset that her man was getting involved.

"EVERYBODY RAISE THE FUCK UP OUT OF HERE, PARTY IS OVER! WE WILL START AT THE SAME TIME TOMMOROW, OUT!" She screamed at the customers as she tried to pull Mason off the bloody man he was still beating. The customers groaned in protest as they left out of the door.

"Baby please, it's enough ok it's enough!" She said to Mayday trying to speak calmly, hoping that he would take her lead and calm down as well. She rubbed his shoulders soothingly, and all I could think of was how much that same affection could have helped me a year ago, when I was raped, bleeding, and upset. Talk about a delayed reaction.

"GET THE FUCK UP AND GET OUT!" Mason yelled at the drunk man.

I rushed out of the room towards my bedroom, to thoroughly check my silent son. He would grow up to be tough because he still hadn't shed one tear. When I made it to the bedroom, I grabbed the first aid kit to clean and dress his wound.

"You are such a strong boy, such a brave boy. Mommy loves

you so much!" I told him as he smiled at me while I continued to check him for any other injuries.

"You could have killed him, baby ain't nobody worth your freedom." I heard my pathetic mother say from the other room.

I don't think I could have hated anyone as much as I hated her in that moment. He disregarded her as he rushed into my bedroom and began to help me check my son.

"Is he hurt badly? I will go back and finish that motherfucker off!" He said angrily. His eyes were on fire and he looked angrier than I had ever seen him.

"Let me see him, let me see him!" My mother said reaching for my now bouncing baby boy.

I knew she was only showing interest because Mayday did. I wanted to feel like she genuinely gave a damn about her grandchild, so I humored her and let her grab my son. I had already bandaged his leg and checked him, but every nerve in my body wanted to snatch her ass up for putting us in this situation in the first place. If she would have kept her word and looked after her grandson or went and cooked for her drunk ass guests *herself* so I could look after my child, my son wouldn't have gotten hurt.

She walked downstairs with him into the kitchen with her cigarette dangling from the side of her painted red lips, and we followed. She put him on the kitchen table while clearing off the loaf of bread, the fake fruit basket, and the ugly place mats. She sat him down and began to look at every inch of him. The bright light bulb beamed down on him and I could tell he was uncomfortable. She turned him around roughly and although he hadn't cried at first, I noticed tears filling his hazel eyes. I think at that point, she'd hurt his feelings more than his body, I couldn't take another second of it.

"Give me my damn baby!" I said snatching him off the table. She was treating him like a turkey about to be stuffed on

Thanksgiving. She treated the turkey better.

"Little girl you are smelling your little ass! Don't talk to me crazy, just because you done had a baby out your little pussy, don't make you a woman!"

"I agree; but protecting him is what makes me a better mama than you could ever be!" I had reached the end of my rope.

I was tired of her treating me like shit, using me to take care of her kids, cook and entertain for her juke joint, and doing everything she was supposed to be doing. The only thing I wasn't doing was screwing Mason. If she kept pushing me that would be next.

As if she had heard my last thought as soon as It was completed, she slapped me, so hard spit flew out of my mouth and my body went into the opposite direction. I didn't drop my child though; I would die before I dropped him. Mason rushed to me to help me up.

"That's enough of this, now. Everybody just a little upset so let's all go and get some rest. We can put the baby to bed and talk in the morning." He said attempting to restore A little peace.

"She can't even handle a hit, little weak ass!" She said triumphantly looking at me. "Now carry your ass upstairs and take care of them kids, get them washed up and ready for bed. You done cut my damn party short, got my man out here fighting, for your little snot nosed-"

Before she could get the rest of the insult out, I put my baby in Mayday's arms and I was on her ass. I punched her in the face with everything in me. I didn't give her a chance to recover from the first hit before I delivered the next few. I hit her anywhere I could, as hard as I could.

I heard feet running down the stairs as my siblings rushed to get me off of her. Where had they been the whole time we were arguing? As much as I did for their asses by being the mother to them that their own mother couldn't, I expected them to have my back.

"Get off mommy, man! You are tripping!" My brother Jean said to me as he grabbed me up off her.

"I can't believe you, Netta!" My sister Edith said.

"Y'ALL DON'T KNOW WHAT THE HELL HAPPENED THOUGH!" I screamed at them with fury.

"SHE LET SOME DRUNK BASTARD TAKE CARE OF MY SON AND HE HURT HIMSELF. LOOK AT MY CHILD'S LEG!! IT'S A BUSY ASS PARKING LOT OUTSIDE OF THIS DOOR WHAT IF HE WOULD HAVE GOTTEN HIT BY A CAR?" I screamed at them while tears flowed freely down my face.

Out of all the years of mean words, torment, and torture, I had never put my hands on my mother. When I became a mother, despite how he was conceived, I no longer loved anyone as much as I loved Wayne. I would die and go to hell for him, and anyone that hurt him would be in hell right beside me.

"She feeling herself cause she got a few licks in." My mother said while standing up and wiping the blood from her nose. She wiped her hand on her baby blue bell bottoms and smiled like a demon.

"The joke is on her though, because I want her and that little bastard of hers out of my house! The minute any child of mine raise their hand up against me they no longer belong to me. It took you long enough bitch!" She said to me laughing like a maniac.

"Now get the hell out!"

Chapter Four
Netta

"Wait, wait you don't have anywhere to go!" Mason said running behind me as I left with the small bag of mine and my son's things.

As if things couldn't get any worse, it was now lightly sprinkling and starting to thunder; it was about to pour down cats and dogs. I had a one year old on my hip, no money, no food for us and no plans. I was screwed.

"Well ain't you Captain Obvious?" I replied to him sarcastically without slowing my stride. With no real destination in mind I wanted to be alone.

"Girl, I'm getting my hair wet running after you, now just hold up!" He said stopping.

I turned around and walked back to him to at least hear him out. I hoped he wasn't chasing me to tell me to go apologize, because I would have rather lay under the bridge by the hospital surrounded by homeless bums, than to let her mistreat my baby and continue to treat me like trash.

"I'm not apologizing!" I told him.

"I don't want you to." He said while licking his sexy lips. I loved when he licked his lips.

"Ok, well what do you want Mason? I have to find somewhere for me and my child for tonight. I can't just stay out here and play with you!" I said while turning and walking away.

He grabbed my arm gently, "You and little man can come and live with me. I would never see you outdoors, Netta." He said sincerely. My heart skipped a beat.

"I don't need you to let me in so you can keep tabs on me for that witch!"

"I'm not letting you in to keep tabs on you for anybody. If you leave, there is no longer anything I need in this house. I have no need to return to it" I looked away as the light rain began to gradually increase its intensity. "Please let me know something. You have me and your son out here in the rain. Just at least stay the night, if you want to leave in the morning then there is no one holding you."

My baby started to cry, and it broke my heart. He didn't ask to be born into this bullshit. My mama once told me that when you became a mother, you would have to do a lot of things you didn't want to for your children. It was just too damn bad that she didn't follow her own advice. It didn't matter how attractive this man was, I had never lived with a man alone; not to mention our huge age difference.

I swallowed my pride and, began to slowly follow him to his car until I noticed a slight movement from the top of our building. I wondered how long my mother had been standing in her bedroom window watching us talk and, my blood began to boil all over again. I put on my big girl face and smiled at her as I walked away twisting my wide hips while rubbing Mason's back with my free hand. I knew we had an audience, so I gave her a show.

His house was beautiful. He lived almost an hour from the hood, in McDonough GA. He even had a two-car garage where his pickup truck sat, loaded with ladders, paint cans, rope, and a bunch of other tools. We walked through the garage into the door leading to his home. The kitchen was a very nice size; the living room was beautifully decorated with earth tones and a large mural painted of him on the wall.

"I'm the King of this castle!" He said to me when he noticed me staring at the mural.

"I can see that." I told him.

I felt dirty and unworthy standing there with my baby on my hip in wet, raggedy clothes and hair that looked like I had been fighting with styling tools. We walked up the stairs directly facing a linen closet. There was a guest bathroom that only contained a toilet, a sink, and a mirror. Continuing down the hallway there was a guest bedroom with only a bed and a small tv. I turned to enter the bedroom, but he grabbed my hand. We continued straight ahead to a closed door at the end of the hallway. He opened the door and the view was breathtaking. Straight ahead was his bed, it was large! On top of his king-sized bed was a gold comforter with matching sheets. To the left of the bed was a large, walk out patio, that overlooked a small lake. To the right of the bed was a large closet. Closer to the door was a huge master bathroom. I walked into the bathroom and there was a huge bathtub.

"We could all fit into this bathtub and, there would still be space left over!" I told him in disbelief. He laughed silently.

"Ok, that's enough touring, can you get the baby cleaned up and fix us something to eat?" He asked sweetly.

I had become so accustomed to my son's weight; I didn't even realize that he was knocked out sleep with his little face in the crook of my neck. Home to him was wherever I was; clearly, he was comfortable. I sat my bag on the floor and walked over to the shower leaning down to turn on the water.

Chapter Five
Netta

"This food ain't hot, this cold! Did you cook it this morning and reheat it or something?" My man asked me with disgust written all over his face.

Mason had walked into the house 45 minutes prior covered in paint; the only time he wasn't glamorous was when he was working. His company Vactor's Remodeling, the construction business he owned with his brother Mensloe, was gifted to them from their father, Clinton Vactor, who died when Mason was 20 and his younger brother was 18. Everyone called his brother M&M for short because of his favorite candy.

"I cooked it this morning." I told him dismissively while continuing to watch the horror movie, Psycho.

This nigga Norman was crazy, and he had my undivided attention. Wayne was crawling around on the floor playing around with a chewable toy and, I was comfortably seated on the thick cushioned couch, with my feet tucked underneath me. A few minutes after Mason walked into the house, and the movie went to commercial break, I hurriedly made him a plate of the leftovers I'd cooked earlier. Silently cursing myself for forgetting to run his bath water. I prayed that he would be too tired to care and, just run it for himself tonight as I hastily put the food on the plate and threw it into the oven on low heat. The fried chicken, rice, and green beans tasted amazing when it was first made, but after sitting on the stove for 12 hours, it had probably lost its fresh, hot taste.

When he finally came downstairs from his shower, shirtless and barefoot, I admired his chocolate skin and his slim muscular body. This man's picture should have been in the dictionary next to the word Blessing. If I knew his parents I would thank them personally. Unfortunately, he never talked to me about them and, about his upbringing. I still had so many questions about where he grew up, what schools he went to, where was his mother, but whenever I would get into those questions, he would change the topic, so I didn't press the issue. What issue I did press was sex. As much as I threw myself at him, he never touched me, and I was beginning to get aggravated. I could walk around the house in nothing but my birthday suit, dripping wet, and he would look all over my ass. I knew this from experience, I tried it. His only response was to get my soaking wet ass off his floors and, find a towel. I laid next to him every night knowing he was getting his sexual needs fulfilled elsewhere.

I felt the pain but, I had no idea where the hit came from because it all happened so quickly. I clutched the back of my head and looked to find the source, when I spotted the broken plate and food scattered on the floor. Wayne looked up at me in surprise temporarily distracted from his toy.

"Why the hell did you do that?!" I asked Mason completely taken aback by what he'd just pulled.

"Bitch, I been out busting my ass all day to pay the bills in this motherfucker!" Mason said angrily, slowly rising from the table.

"You been sitting IN MY HOUSE on your stankin ass, watching MY tv, eating MY food, relaxing in MY heat; you and your child! Do you have any idea how hard I go for this shit?" he asked now face to face with me and, looking into my eyes. He looked like an angry lion ready to pounce at any second if I uttered the wrong words. I was terrified.

"I. I – I'm sorry, Mason." I stuttered with tears falling from my eyes, as I heard Norman Bates on the movie talking to his mother.

"Yeah, you are sorry. You knew from the get-go that when I got here, I would be hungry. Every night you have a hot plate for me and, don't think I didn't notice that my water wasn't ran. So, what's up Little Girl? What, are you tired of being here? You miss your mama's house? ain't shit changed over there, she ready for you to come running back home with your tail tucked, ready to do everything she wants you to do while she treats you like dog shit on the bottom of her shoe!

You know what? Go grab y'all shit, I'm about to take both of y'all asses to your mother's. I'm out here being a good man, providing a home and taking care of you and a child that aint even mine. Ain't no sorry woman about to lay around in my house all day!" He said angrily, grabbing his keys off the kitchen countertop and heading towards the door of the garage.

"May no...... Please!!" I dropped down to my knees begging him.

My son's toy was digging in my skin something awful, but I was plastered in that spot. The tears flowed freely as I ignored another verbal warning my mother had given, NEVER let a man see you cry. I didn't understand why I kept hearing her words at my lowest moments. I disregarded her words yet again because, If she had provided a decent home, I wouldn't be on my knees crying and begging a man for a place to stay. I loved living and raising Wayne here with Mason. His house was so peaceful and a far cry from the chaos I had grown up in; all night parties, picking my mother up from the floor when she was higher than a kite, slaving over a stove for hours, taking care of my younger siblings, even after I had a child of my own.

"I mean, you act like a nigga asking too much from you Netta!"

"No, you don't ask a lot. I was lazy, I'm sorry. I can do better and I will!"

He stood near the door with an aggravated expression, like he still wasn't convinced that I could be useful to him. So, I had to show him how useful I could be. I crawled over to him slowly, he watched me like he was speculating my next move. When I made it to his feet, I bowed my head and kissed them both. Now on my knees and face to face with his pelvis I reached for his pants, he grabbed my wrist.

"What are you doing?" Mason asked me nonchalantly and unimpressed.

"I'm going to make you happy, so that you will keep us." I replied while looking up at him.

"Hmmmp," He replied with a side smile and walked out of the door leaving me on my knees, looking at the door like a puppy waiting for his master to return.

I felt humiliated and belittled. I dropped my head in my hands and continued to cry while rubbing on my throbbing head. I knew there would be a lump there in a few hours. I felt my son tug me and, I looked down at his big beautiful smile. He assumed that since I was on the floor, I was about to play with him. Even though I felt like shit I didn't want to disappoint the only other person I truly cared for so, that is exactly what I did. Despite Mason throwing him up in my face, I knew my son wasn't a burden, he was my blessing. Wayne was my reason for living, and my gift from God, to constantly remind me that he hadn't given up on me no matter what my circumstances looked like.

After playing with my little boy then giving him a hot bath, he fell into a deep slumber. I put him in bed then returned downstairs to the living room. I started with cleaning up the food and shattered glass from the plate. Afterwards, I stored the remaining food from earlier that day in the refrigerator. Even though he felt he was too good to eat the leftovers I was raised on survival, so I would eat whatever necessary.

I then thawed the pork steaks and cleaned the kitchen

thoroughly. After they were ready to cook, I soaked them, seasoned them and put them in the oven. I made my famous Mac and Cheese recipe from scratch, with rice, and put some buttered dinner rolls in the oven. After his meal was completed, I fixed him a plate fit for a King and placed it in the oven so it would stay warm.

Chapter Six
<u>Netta</u>

♪ When a man loves a woman
Can't keep his mind on nothing else
He'll trade the world
For the good thing he's found
If she's bad he can't see it
She can do no wrong
Turn his back on his best friend
If he put her down ♪

The feeling of his thick wet tongue woke me up. He sucked on my pussy lips like they were the last set of lips he would ever kiss; I felt the quick burst of a foreign sensation come all over my body. The sweet bliss was the equivalent of being at the top of a rollercoaster and then plummeting down face first. I had never felt something so amazing. I didn't give a damn if his lips had been on my mama, the next-door neighbor, or hell even the mail lady's coochie he was mine now and that was all that mattered to me. I loved Mason and everything about him, and I had been waiting for this moment for months.

He placed one more long, gentle, suckle on my sweet spot and my legs began to shake. Maybe he sensed that he was giving me more than I could handle, because he moved his kisses outward, to my inner thigh. He kissed and nibbled without urgency, like he had all night. His patience was becoming unnerving. He kissed my hip softly and I felt tingling in my lower back.

"Mmmh," I heard myself moan deeply.

He looked up at me from between my legs and licked his lips. I felt my stomach doing back flips. I tried to squeeze my thighs together to relieve the throbbing in between them but, he was currently in between them; there was nothing I could do but take this sweet torture. He used his big hands to massage my ass cheeks as he continued to punish me with soft sucks and gentle tugs. I threw my head back in ecstasy and, began to grind my pelvis into his face. My hips started to move in their own rhythm.

He stopped abruptly, I looked down to see what happened; he was staring at me with a weird expression.

"Di- did I do something wrong?" I stuttered. I flashed back to earlier and instantly touched the bruise on my head from the plate. I didn't want to upset him.

"Don't move!" He replied in a low deep voice. So, even though it took everything in me to stay still, I did as I was told.

With my thighs still in his hands, he began to kiss on my stomach, up to my breast. Taking my nipple into his mouth, he gently sucked and tugged at it. He kissed my neck softly and released my right leg, he used his now free hand to rub in between my thighs.

"Look at me!" He demanded to me in that same deep lust filled voice. My eyes opened slowly to find him staring at me intensely.

I took a deep calming breath as I felt his finger do what mine had done a million times; It felt so much better when he did it. He inserted one finger inside of me as deep as it would go; my eyes closed, and my back arched. I bit my lip to keep from screaming out when his one, thick finger, turned into 2 fingers. I lifted my torso and placed my head in the curve of his neck. He removed his fingers and sucked my juices before using his now free hand to pull the back of my shoulder blade down on my back, gently. He kissed my lips hungrily to distract me from the fact that he was trying to insert his thick, dick into the place it was supposed to go.

"Mayyyyyyyyyyy!" I moaned his name softly into his ear while holding him tightly.

"I love you; you hear me? I know you feel me inside, nothing and no one else matters. It's just us baby; we all that matter." He told me and I believed him.

Mason made love to me all night. Even when my baby woke up from the other room and cried for me, I didn't move. I continued to let Mason have my body, my soul, my mind, and my spirit. I was his and nothing and no one else mattered. I had never felt so loved in my life.

Two years later

The sound of my throw up hitting the porcelain toilet confirmed what I already knew. I had been through this process before, so I knew it wasn't a stomach bug. I was pregnant, again. I wasn't sure how far along I was, but I had only missed one period, so I was guessing around six weeks. The baked chicken, yellow rice, and dinner rolls were all coming up in chunks, when I felt my toddler pull at the hemline of the bottom of my shirt. Since he had learned how to crawl, he was all over the house, and I had to keep an eye on him even more now that he was mobile.

"MA, juice!" Wayne said to me while tugging on me to get my attention. He always wanted some damn juice; I was about to start giving his spoiled butt some water.

"OK papa, mommy is going to get you some juice." I said to him, standing on my wobbly legs trying to control the dizziness. I made it downstairs barely, before I heard banging at the door.

BAM.BAM.BAM!

I didn't know if the banging was in my head or real life until I looked down at Wayne and saw him looking at the door. *So, it's real?* I thought to myself. I walked over to the door using all the strength I had and pulled it open. She stood a little shorter than me, but the first thing I noticed was her beautiful face. I could tell she wasn't all the way African American and had some Mexican or Cuban in her. Her long, wavy hair flowed loosely framing her plump face. Her dimples were deep enough to where they were noticeable, even without her smiling. She looked so angry that, if looks could kill my ass would have been 8ft under. Buried six feet and, knocked down an extra two.

"Can I help you with anything?" I asked not in the mood for the bullshit.

"You sure can, lil young hoe!"

"Wait, what the hell is your problem lady, who are you?"

"I'm Mason's wife!" She said holding her left hand a few inches from my face, as if she needed to be that close for me to see the rock on her ring finger. "As well as the mother of his child!" she continued, pointing down to what I now noticed was a slightly protruding belly. She wore her pregnancy well, with a beautiful long flowing dress that couldn't, hide the fact that she had hips for days.

Married. How was he married? I lived in his house, there was no way in the hell he was married to this lady.

"He can't be married he lives here with me; we've been living together for a year and a half. You clearly have the wrong nigga." I told her with my hand on my hip.

She laughed loudly.

"Wrong nigga?! Wrong nigga! So, Mason Vactor, Mayday for short; about yay high," she said curving her blinging wrist to describe his height. "thin but muscular, dark chocolate skin, thick full lips, can dress his ass off, has multiple cars but mostly drives a baby blue Cadillac Eldorado, that I bought him for his birthday! Still sound like the wrong nigga?" she asked me, stepping closer in my face.

I didn't want to knock the pregnant bitch out, especially while I was sure that I was pregnant as well, so I decided to take the high road.

"Look Lady-"

"Lisa, my name is not lady, little girl!"

"I'm not going to be too many more little girls, Lisa. Clearly, I didn't know anything about you, so why do you feel it's ok to attack another woman who had no idea of your existence, versus the man that you married, that pledged his life to you, that clearly knows you exist?! You're not upset with him, but you're upset with me?"

I could tell that what I told her caught her off guard. If I would have given in to her antics, we would've both be rolling around in the street, one blow from a miscarriage and a jail cell.

"Come inside, Please. Let's just talk this out like women; this really is my first time, hearing any of this." I told her sincerely.

I was trying so hard not to break down; Mason was literally all I had. He hadn't been home in a few days, and he had his times where he would disappear for long periods of times, but I never accused him of anything. I didn't want to be like other women and run him away with nagging and lack of trust. Whenever he did come home, I treated him like the King he was. Hot meals were prepared daily, his bath water was always, ran around the same time every day and if he didn't come home to eat or take the bath, me and Wayne would usually just eat the food and use the bath water.

She gave me a nasty look and walked inside of the house.

"Would you like anything to drink?" I asked her, putting on the bravest face I had, but I knew as soon as she walked out of the door, my emotional flood gates would ravage some shit.

"Evian. I know you have some, it's the only thing he drinks if he isn't drinking alcohol. He doesn't mess around with tap." she said as if she knew the man that I was madly in love with. She wasn't wrong.

I walked to the fridge and grabbed her a water bottle while she sat on one of the island bars stools, in the center of the kitchen.

"It even smells like him in here." She said clearly getting aggravated all over again.

"What's making the fact that you didn't know hard to believe, is how calm you are right now. I know you've been fucking with him about a year and some change, I've been married to him for 3 years. That man was my first everything, and whenever it's a new lil hoe he is sniffing after, I see the changes in him." she said with her Mexican accent coming out. She spoke perfect English, so, I assumed when she was angry enough, her roots showed.

"Im just trying to be calm right now, Lisa." I told her. "Inside I'm a mess. I was raped to create my son; Mason is the first man I have ever *willingly* let inside of me. I love him I can't lie and, I want to feel like this is just all a messed-up dream. Yes, as you keep stating, I am young; I'm turning 18 the end of this year."

"Lord, you're younger than I thought!" she said holding her hand to her chest. "Este bastardo negro bajo sucio!" she said while putting her face in her hands.

"Did you just call me a nigger?" I asked her, rolling my neck. I tried to be cordial, but the burrito eating hoe wasn't about to sit there and disrespect me either.

"No!" she said holding up one of her perfectly manicured hands.

"I'm currently directing my anger towards him as you suggested but, if you want me to throw it back at you" she said giving me a nasty look and I threw my hands up in surrender.

"My only question for you is, if you knew about me and you know he's done this, before, what took you so long to approach me AND, why do *you* stay?" I asked her.

"You're not the only one that loves him sweetheart. I turn a blind eye to shit because I built that man; he had nothing when we met. That was until I found some mail in his car with this address, a further investigation led me to fund out that he owned this damn house. Cheating I have dealt with, but this disrespect right here is next level. It was my father that gave him money for the company. My father taught him everything he knows about the construction and remodeling business. We moved here with nothing and my father started off as a regular worker for a construction company. Hungry to learn the business, he got under the owner and learned everything he knew. He then learned the business aspect of it and went into business for himself. He had plenty of workers because he sent for some men from our family back home, to come and work for him. He began to get all of the contracts for the city as well as the state, because he was willing to bid lower than his competition plus get the work done fast and well." she said pausing to take a sip of her water bottle.

"When I met Mason, he didn't have a damn thing; *NADA!*" she said swiping her hand under her neck in a cutting motion. "My father was against it from the start, but I fought for our relationship. Eventually my father gave in and because he wanted me to continue to have the fine things in life, he taught Mason the business."

"I was told he and his brother inherited their business from his father" I told her in disbelief. She laughed out loud and, banged her hand on the countertop.

"You mean his alcoholic father? The father that Mason told *ME* beat his mother faithfully until he killed her with his bare hands, right in front of Mason and his Mensloe? Get the hell out of here." she said angrily.

"Look," I told her feeling dumber by the minute. It seemed that the only thing that was true about him that I knew, was the fact that he had a brother. If she hadn't described everything about my man, I would have for sure felt like she was talking about someone else.

"Mason took me in when my mother kicked me out; I have

nothing but him. If I leave this house right now, I don't even know where I would go. I have no family, education, skills, a three-year-old and another baby inside of me. So, I wouldn't exactly say that I have a lot of options right now. That is why I just try to keep Mason happy and not ask a lot of questions."

"You're pregnant?" she asked me sadly.

"Yes, I am." I told her sadly and placing my hand protectively on my flat stomach. I knew that I wouldn't start showing until later in the pregnancy. That was how I was able to hide Wayne from my mother for so long.

She got off the stool like she was about to put her hands on me, but suddenly had a better idea.

"You know what, I'm done!" she said. "Since you have nothing without him, I am going to give him to you. I'm going to give you the ass whooping's you can't tell anyone about because even though he is hurting you, you *still* want to protect him. You can have the other women approaching you; being the laughing stock of the city, the debt, the frequent clinic trips, the manipulation, all of it!!!" she said while looking me eye to eye. "I pray that you can handle it and, you don't end up like his mother!" She said before turning around and walking out the door.

I collapsed onto the floor and, cried until my throat was dry. My head was throbbing, and every muscle in my body hurt from being on the floor for so long. I didn't care about feeding my son, I didn't care about getting him the juice he wanted, I didn't care about his cries, all I could do was lay in that spot and wait for Mason.

He came home that night, picked me up from the floor and put me into the bed. He was home now, so I never mentioned that his wife stopped by. I didn't want to upset him.

Chapter Seven
<u>Netta</u>

♫ If being right, means being without you
Then I'd rather live a wrong doing life.
Your mama and daddy say it's a shame
It's a downright disgrace
Long as I got you by my side
I don't care what your people say ♫

"Stomp that pretty hoe!" The girl screamed out to her friend as she held my hair down, to keep me in place for the other girl to dig her boot into my face.

"Bitch think you cute, you think you good, Huh? Everybody getting that dick. That's my dick, my friend dick, the city dick!" She said as she continued to kick me.

I felt my tooth loosen up as the blows to my face continued. I felt another girl punching other parts of my body while one girl held me down, and the other girl kicked me in the face. My three kids screamed and cried on the sideline, but I couldn't get to them. I felt the blood running down my face and I felt my eye beginning to swell. I just prayed that it would be over soon, because that was all I could do.

Before my current situation of being stomped into the pavement, I was out with the kids. My son wanted to push the newest addition to the family, his baby sister Bonnie, in the stroller. My oldest daughter Terri at 2 years old, wanted to do everything her big brother did. We had just gone to JC Penny to take family pictures. Mason couldn't make it because he had to work, but I knew that most of the time when he said he had to work, it was the code for he had to go be with another woman.

I was no longer the naïve little girl that Mason had rescued from her mother, whom felt like he was a God on earth. At this point I just tried to keep my man happy and raise his children as best as I could. I knew he was cheating and the frequent trips to the clinic confirmed that. Within the years of being with Mason I had contracted Gonorrhea, Syphilis, and Chlamydia, twice. He was the only man I had ever been with, so I knew the diseases weren't coming from me. The fact that he'd stuck me with two more kids, given me multiple diseases, demanded that I give him my entire pay check from my housekeeping job at the hotel, and rearranged my face often, had me as afraid to be without him as I was to be with him. I was excited that this week he allowed me to keep enough of my paycheck to buy outfits and a pair of shoes for the kids and myself, as well as enough to pay for these family pictures.

One of my coworkers had gone to take family pictures and, come back to the job raving and showing off the pictures of her boyfriend standing behind her as she sat in the big wooden chair holding their son on her lap. They were all dressed in the same colors, and the picture had a nice beach background behind them. The pictures came in huge sizes to put on the wall or even key chain sizes to keep on your key. As I worked the rest of my shift, I realized that I didn't have any pictures of me and, my kids. I had gotten jealous and came home that night begging Mason to allow us to do the same thing. He said no.

I talked about it for weeks, until I convinced Mayday to let us go. We decided on a Friday so, I took an off day from work, woke my boo up with a big appreciation breakfast, and gave it to him while he was in bed. After me and the kids got dressed in our matching Purple short set outfits, we waited patiently while he put on his bell bottom jeans, his purple silk shirt that exposed his sexy chest hair, and his matching purple alligator shoes. He wouldn't let me get my hair straightened out, so it sat in a nappy ponytail on top of my head. Thankful, that he had given in and, deciding not to sweat the small stuff, I did the girl's hair to match mine. I decided to tell my coworkers that I wanted me and my daughters to look exactly alike so, I wore my hair like that intentionally. Mason would be the best dressed person on the picture, but that was fine. He was the King of our castle and the King of our lives; it was ok if he looked the best.

When we made It downtown, I suggested that Mason park next to one of the meters. He told me that he didn't need to park because he couldn't stay.

"What you mean you ain't staying?" I asked him angrily and shocked. We had gone out and chosen these outfits together, I paid for everything with the portion he let me keep, and I was really looking forward to this family picture. I knew he didn't dress like this for work and, if he wasn't staying for the pictures, I wanted to know where the hell he was going.

WHACKKKK!!

He slapped me so fast I didn't realize I'd gotten slapped, until I wiped the blood away from my lip.

"I only meant," I started.

"It doesn't matter what the hell you meant! Do you stand or sit down to take a piss?" He asked me as if he didn't know the answer.

"I sit down." I said putting my hand close to my face, so that I could try to block the next blow.

"Yeah, but you see me, I stand up; I'm a standup guy. I'm a man. I'm THE MAN! I take care of ya'll, don't question me Netta!"

"That's right, I'm sorry May. Can you give me money so I can pay for the pictures for me and the kids?" I asked him while flinching and praying that he didn't hit me again in front of the kids. I hated when he hit me in front of them.

"Here you go." He said handing me a twenty-dollar bill.

"If you can't pay for it with this, then don't get it!" He told me.

"Thank you." I replied, before stepping out of the Gold Cadillac he had just bought.

I went to the backseat to get the kids out and Wayne looked at me with tears rolling down his face. He had been around this abuse since he was baby, so I expected him to be used to it. Yet, every time it happened, I would catch him crying, silently. I wiped his tears discreetly and kissed his forehead. I grabbed the car seat and the stroller out of the backseat.

"Don't run in the street, stand right here next to me" I told Terri.

I didn't have to tell Wayne because he wouldn't leave my side; he was a true mama's boy. I assembled the stroller as quickly as I could, because I could sense Mason's frustration with waiting. When I was done, I shut the car door gently being sure not to slam it.

"I will swing back around in a few hours. Have fun." Mason said before hitting the car horn twice and pulling back into traffic.

Determined not to let him destroy my day with my babies, we did just that. Walking into the picture place, I pulled the front desk woman aside.

"How much is the cheapest package of pictures you have?" I asked her.

"Well the price list is right here." She said, walking towards the desk I had just pulled her away from, grabbing a sheet of laminated paper and handing it to me.

"I. I can't read that; I don't have my glasses with me." I lied.

"Oh ok, well the cheapest package we have is 10.99 for 9 pictures of one pose." She said. "These are the sizes of the 9 pictures. One poster size, four of the five by eight, people usually give these ones away to family and friends, two wallet size, and two key chain size." She said looking at me.

"Ok, well I will take that package!" I told her handing over the twenty-dollar bill.

"Great choice" she said to me, "now select what background you want, then have a seat over there" she said pointing. After choosing a different background than my coworker, I sat down in front of the camera in the straw chair and, put my newborn daughter in my lap. Wayne stood on one side of me, and Terri stood on the opposite side.

"SMILE, on three!" The camera man said to us before counting down and snapping the picture.

When we received the pictures, I didn't have to fake being happy anymore because it was now genuine. We all looked so nice and everyone was smiling; even my newborn cracked a smile for the camera.

"Ya'll did soooo good!" I told my babies getting down on my knees to get eye level with them. I kissed them, and stood back up to assemble the stroller, when four girls walked into the studio.

"Heyyy, Net!" One of the girls said to me while smiling big. I remembered her from the neighborhood, we had gone to school together for the little time I did go.

"Hey, how you been?" I asked her, smiling. I didn't get much female interaction outside of work, since that was the only place Mayday allowed me to go.

"I been good. Your kids are adorable!" She said looking down at my kids.

I noticed one of the girls she walked into the studio with was looking at me with a confused expression. It was as if she couldn't remember where she knew me from. I saw her facial expression change from uncertainty to anger, when it seemed like she finally realized why I looked familiar to her. She turned her back and stood in front of the other two girls and told something to them.

"How old are they?" asked the girl, who I remembered was named Helen.

"My boy is the oldest, he's five." I said looking down at him and smiling. "My girls are two and 5 months."

"Oh ok, what are their names?"

"Wayne, Terri, and Bonnie." I replied.

I began to have a bad, gut feeling about the situation, so I grabbed for Wayne's hand and began to walk away

"It was nice seeing you again after all these years." I told her.

"So, are all of these Mayday's kids? Or is what your mama saying about you around the neighborhood true? were you just out fucking off on everybody and don't know who the daddies are?" Helen asked me with a smirk.

So, the bitch was just being nosey like I suspected. I thought. A familiar face didn't always mean it was a friendly face. Maybe I didn't see her as an enemy because I knew I had never done anything wrong to her or said anything out the way about her.

"My mama is a lying bitch and that's all I got to say about that!" I said heading towards the door.

That's when I felt my ponytail being yanked in the opposite direction. My daughter's stroller slipped out of my hands, but it didn't roll out of the door because the door shut so quickly.

"Mommy!" my son screamed and reached for me.

"WHAT THE FUCK?!" I screamed as I snatched away from one of the girls, who was with the group.

"NO, NO, there will be none of that in here! Take that stuff up the street to, wherever the hell y'all stay; this is a business!" said the lady who told me the price and details of the picture packages.

"My bad, Selma!" Helen said. "We didn't mean any harm; we will take this outside."

I looked at them all like they were crazy. I wasn't leaving out of that door to get jumped on by a bunch of girls I didn't know, for reasons I didn't know. This shit was crazy! I could see why Mason wanted me to just stay in the house!

"Look, I'm not sure what the problem is but, I don't even know ya'll or the reason ya'll have a problem with me." I said to them. "I have my babies with me, I'm not trying to fight nobody or start no trouble."

"You told MayDay to stop fucking with me, bitch!" said the girl who I assumed was the leader. "He came to my house a few nights ago and said I gave him the Clap, and that you made him choose between me and you. Since you the mother of his kids, he's choosing you! I didn't know if it was you for sure because he keeps your ass locked away like you Cinderella in the tower. Bitch you ain't special! I'm finer than you, and I know plenty of other girls that's finer than you too!" she said with her hand on her hip.

Her ass was probably 100 pounds soaking wet, and I knew she only had so much shit to talk because she had a group of yes girls behind, ready to do whatever she told them to.

"Look, I don't know you, so I can't tell him to choose between me and you. What I do know is, he gave me Gonorrhea and I told him if he wanted to keep fucking with different nasty hoes in the street, he could have them, but I wouldn't be here. I'm tired of taking trips to the free clinic. I know it ain't me I'm faithful!" I said trying to get them to understand where I was coming from so they wouldn't jump me.

"Well, you about to get a nasty hoe in the street ass whooping; he left me because of you!" she said rushing to me and hitting me squarely in my face.

She did everything so suddenly, I didn't have time to think, only react. I lunged into her like a cheetah catching squirrel and, went to town on her thin ass. I was getting the best of her, until I felt some hands grab my hair and snatch me backwards. When the other friend jumped in, that gave all of them the greenlight to go to town on my ass. I was getting hit with everybody part known to man, including elbows, knees, and feet. It felt like one of the girls even spit on me.

I eventually gave up on fighting back because I was outnumbered. I just prayed my babies were ok and that it would end eventually.

"That's community dick, all of us done fucked him!" said the girl that I started fighting initially.

She was now punching me in the face with all her might while Helen held my hair, wrapped around her fist to keep my head steady, and the other two girls held my arms back.

"The police are on their way so go ahead and have fun, because they are coming!" said the front desk lady. She made sure to stand back behind the equipment, so she wouldn't catch a stray blow that was meant for me.

"MAMA!" my two-year-old screamed; I had never felt so defenseless. There I was again going through some shit not brought on by something I did, but because of Mason's ass.

WHHHHIRRRHHH!

When they heard the sirens, they let me go, and took off out the back door of the store. No longer having the strength to stand all I could do was fall to my knees as my son pushed his baby sister in the stroller and, ran up to me with my daughter Terri right behind him. My lips felt swollen and, I felt blood running down the side of my face, as the officer walked into the studio.

"What the hell?!" he said when he laid eyes on me.

The officer that arrived at the scene looked young I was that his baby face got him out of a lot of situations. He looked to be in his early twenties and stood around 6 '5 or 6'6, because he towered over everyone in the room. His extremely, light complexion would have earned him the nick name high yellow or maybe even White Boy in the hood. He was clean cut, with the just got out of the academy haircut and his eyes were hazel. You could get lost in them if you allowed yourself to. His uniform fitted his toned physique and his presence commanded respect, like my baby Mayday. Everyone knew my baby didn't take no shit.

"56 to Radio."

"Radio, Go Ahead."

"I need a 10-52 to JC Penny's photography studio in the back of the department store, Downtown Atlanta zip code 30310." the policeman said through his walkie talkie. "I have a young woman, early 20's, African American, a significant amount of facial damage; looks like she has been physically attacked. I also have three children with the young woman, one of them an infant."

"10-4, ambulance in Route." the dispatcher replied.

"Hello ma'am, I'm officer Peddle Way." the officer told me while reaching for his notepad. So, tell me what happened here."

"Nothing officer. Just had a disagreement with a few girlfriends, I'm fine." I said attempting to stand fully but wincing from the pain and leaning back over.

"If it hurts your midsection when you stand fully, that is a sign of cracked ribs." he said to me while looking at me with pity.

"Ok, so you're not a snitch, you will deal with it when

you get back to the hood, because it's the code of the streets." he said using air quotes when he said code. "I don't understand why people are always condoning this kind of foolishness. You would rather take matters into your own hands then, the moment you get hurt or you hurt somebody, while your ass is behind bars, people want to yell, *Free Pookie* or *Free Day Day*, and act like the police are corrupt and the problem. Talk to me and let me get the people that hurt you off the streets, before they do this again to another girl."

"I'm sorry officer but, it's not like that." I told him while easing into a chair because I could no longer stand. "These girls jumped me because I don't want to share my man with them. They are throwing out and picking up diseases like it ain't no thang. I gave my man an ultimatum to choose between them or me. He loves me and his kids, so he chose me. They got upset about that like it's my fault that I'm a good woman, and he chose me, so they jumped on me."

"A real man wouldn't put you in the position where you have to give him an ultimatum to cheat or be faithful to you. You don't deserve that. Love shouldn't hurt or in this case it shouldn't get you hurt." the pretty boy officer said to me.

"I mean haters are going to hate, officer. I'm not letting my man go because that is exactly what these women want me to do, so they can have him to themselves. My man is sexy, he has a nice body, nice house, nice cars, nice clothes. I just look at it like this is the price I have to pay for having someone like him." I shrugged.

"You're going to end up in a nice body bag because of his shenanigans." the man said with aggravation, before walking out the door to greet the medics whom had just arrived.

"I don't need an ambulance, I'm fine." I told the medic as they rushed in the door with the officer right behind them, as I struggled to inhale and exhale completely. They pulled out their equipment and attempted to get me to lie down on a large cardboard, like I had been in a car accident.

"I'm not laying on that thing, I'm not getting in the ambulance, and I'm for damn sure not going to the hospital! I'm not doing it!" I said

"So, you are refusing medical attention ma'am, that is what you are saying to me?" the medic asked while looking for a form for me to sign, confirming that I didn't want to go to the hospital.

"Yes, I am ref.." I didn't get a chance to finish my sentence before the Officer jumped in.

"If you don't go to the hospital, I'm taking you to jail for Disorderly conduct, disturbing the peace, and assault because you were fighting." he said.

"That is a bunch of bullsh-"

"Say it, go ahead and say it so I can add on a resisting arrest charge. These are your kids am I right? Yeah, you are going to jail, and they are going straight into the system, so you just go ahead and say it!"

I shut my mouth immediately and looked the other way. You had to know when to hold them and when to fold them.

"Ok, what do you want me to do, man? I'm tired, my kids are tired and hungry!" I said to him angrily.

"Just get checked out and let them see if you are seriously injured. I will be on the way to the hospital right behind you with the adorable kids. Officer Peddle Way may stop and grab them some happy meals and ice cream cones from McDonalds. How does Happy Meals and ice cream cones sound kids?" he asked them as he turned from me and squatted down to be eye level with my two kids. He had the sweetest smile.

"Yayyyyyy!" the kids answered in agreement.

This was the main reason children needed an adult present; you say something about some ice cream and, their little greedy behinds start bouncing off the walls to get in your car. When we made it home, I would have the stranger talk with them again. I didn't care if this was a cop, a uniform alone wasn't a sole judge of character.

"Ok, Grady Memorial is the closest and McDonald's is right next to it, so it shouldn't take you guys too long." I said grimacing from the pain, while flashing him a glare. "I will take Bonnie and you two," I said turning to the kids. "Mommy needs you to be on your best, best, behavior for the nice policeman, Officer Peddle Way ok?"

I stooped down the best I could, and I felt winded and a lightning pain start from my side and cover my entire body. This shit felt worse than childbirth, something had to be wrong. I kept a brave face as I gave my babies forehead kisses. My son stood on his tip toes and, whispered in my ear "I won't tell him about daddy being mean to you." then he kissed me on my cheek.

My rib pain didn't make my eyes fill with water, but his statement did; my little boy was very smart for his age. He heard me say enough times that whatever happened in the house stayed in the house, but the fact that he was only 5 years old and he knew not to give out the wrong information despite who asked or what they offered, proved to me that he had my back. I knew then that he always would.

With the help of the medic, I struggled to get into the back of the ambulance. When we pulled away and headed to the E.R., I wondered why the hell Mason hadn't pulled up yet. It had been hours and he was nowhere to be found. Maybe if he would have been there, I wouldn't have been sitting in an ambulance and my babies wouldn't be in the backseat of a damn police car.

Maybe he could have talked some sense into his hoes to stop them from jumping me.

Chapter Eight
Netta

♫ How can a loser ever win?
Please help me mend my broken heart and let me live again

I can still feel the breeze that rustles through the trees
And misty memories of days gone by
We could never see tomorrow, no one said a
word about the sorrow ♫

After a week of Mason not coming home, I began to get worried. I didn't know what bills were due, or how much, they would be to pay because I couldn't read the notices being sent. Even if I could read the notices, I couldn't afford to pay the bills. Every dime I ever made I gave to Mason, and I wouldn't get any other money any time soon because I couldn't go back to work for 6 weeks. I didn't know what to do, I immediately fell into a deep depression. I couldn't eat, sleep, or think; the only positive thing about the situation was the fact that my boss Ms. Arlene, knew I was a very hard worker, so she agreed to hold my job for 6 weeks, while I healed.

For the entire six weeks I survived with my children. I began to borrow from neighbors when my daughter ran out of milk. By the grace of God, the woman next door had a newborn as well. The first disconnection was the gas. We no longer had hot water but since we still had electricity, I could boil water on the stove for hot baths and still cook. The second disconnection was the house phone. I could do without it because it wasn't like I talked to anyone other than my boss, who called to check on me regularly. I rationed the food so it would stretch but it was getting incredibly low, still I fed my children; they never went hungry even if I had to.

When I woke up in the middle of the night and flicked the light switch, I immediately began to panic. I ran through the house flipping every switch, knowing what happened already. The lights had been disconnected. We had plenty of candles so I used them at night, so me and the kids wouldn't be in complete darkness. Whenever my mother's lights were disconnected, she would tell me that people knew when you were outside or didn't have a place to live, but they didn't know when you didn't have electricity. Again, her words coming at my lowest point, I used her words for strength to get me through, even if I couldn't stand her.

The very next morning I knocked on the neighbor's door. I begged her to let me run an outdoor extension cord through her back door so that me and the kids would have access to the microwave to warm food and water for washups, as well as, one lamp and the tv. I told her that I couldn't read so I didn't know when the bills were due or how much they cost. She felt sorry for me and, agreed to help me out in any way she could. I hated that I had to be out of work instead of making money to care for me and my children.

WELCOME BACK!

The banner read in the basement, conference room of my job. On various tables there were snacks, finger foods, and juice; they even went to buy me a cake with my name written on it. Tears immediately filled my eyes. No one, not even my mother, had ever done something so nice for me before. The entire housekeeping staff, the floor men, the laundry attendants, and my supervisor, all told me how much they missed me and, how glad they were that I was back and healthy.

"You gave us a scare there, child!" Ms. Moreen told me in her thick New Orleans Accent. She had been employed there the longest and, she was always so sweet to me. She was like a grandmother to me and always kept it real with me whenever I asked her advice on anything, personal or professional.

"Yeah, I thought you weren't coming back." said Julio, the grounds man.

"Well she's here now, so you all eat up and relax for this next hour, then it's back to scheduled programming; we have a hotel to keep up. It wouldn't run so smoothly without us." said Ms. Arlene, my boss, while turning her attention on me and smiling adoringly. She had become the closest thing I'd ever had to a mother. The only reason I didn't want to ask for her help with my home situation, was because she would tell me the same thing, she told me a thousand times; leave Mason. She spoke from experience, telling me of all the horror stories she had gone through with the father of her children. She told me about how he abused her mentally, physically, and verbally in the worst ways that he could think of. The stories she told me were terrible and Mason had never done the terrible things her ex, husband had done to her. I found myself wondering how she stayed; I also found myself wondering why it was so easy to see the solution to her problems while I couldn't figure out how to solve my own.

I met Ms. Arlene before I started working for her. Me and Mayday were out at Big Bear grocery store because he wanted me to make him some chitlins, cornbread, macaroni and cheese, and roast; we didn't have any of the ingredients. Usually he went to the store alone, grabbed the ingredients, then brought them home to me to be cooked; he was a little off to me this day though. His eyes were bloodshot red, he kept moving his mouth in a chewing motion, but he didn't have any gum or any food around. He also had a nervous twitch that I'd never witnessed before.

"Are you ok baby?" I asked him when he woke me up out of my sleep and told me to get dressed, because he wanted me to ride to the grocery store with him.

"Yeah, yeah." he said rapidly "I'm good, I'm straight, just hurry the hell up, I want some roast, and- and some chitlins with macaroni."

"Babe, it's going to take forever for me to make chitlins, that's all-day and-"

WHACCCKKKKKKKKKKKKKK!

His backhand threw me right back on the bed I'd just gotten out of. My face stung and tears burned the back of my eyes, as I tried to avoid eye contact with him; I would never learn.

"Now, now, now, I said what I said!" he said talking fast.

"Ok." I said getting back up quickly, putting on the first thing I could get my hands on. I had never seen him like this, and I didn't know what he would do, so I obeyed.

"Let me just go grab the kids." I said in fear, heading towards the other room.

He snatched me back by my shirt and slammed me on the ground like a wrestler. The impact took my breath away and I struggled to inhale. He put his large hand on my nose and mouth, at the same time, to stop my breathing while he pinned me down with his weight. The only thing I could do was wiggle back and forth and turn my head from side to side, as I attempted to breathe. I looked into his blood shot eyes; they were as wide as I'd ever seen them. He smiled down at me and drool ran from his lips onto my cheek. I began to see dark spots and my head felt like it was about to explode, before he removed his hand.

"UUUUUUUUUGHHHH!" I took a huge deep breath in. I took in too much air at once and I began to cough uncontrollably as my body convulsed; it was the worst feeling I ever felt. This man truly was a monster.

"Did I tell ya stankin ass to get them kids? Huh, huh?" he said getting close enough to my face to kiss me, while tiny droplets of spit flew into my eyes.

"I'm tired of looking at those damn kids, leave they ass here. Leave em here!" He said while getting off me and standing back to his feet.

"I can't leave my kids here with Wayne, he is 4 years old!" I said crying and hoping he would understand. He could do what he wanted to do to me, but two of those kids were his kids as well.

"They're your daughters, MAY! Your daughters, your little girls." I said to him while sobbing, getting on my knees in front of him. I clasped my hands together as If I were praying to god and, I begged him. "Please, please don't make me leave them, I don't want to leave them!" He looked down at me with disgust.

"Get your dramatic ass up and grab them then! But leave your nappy head ass son! Leave his ass, you got raped and got pregnant with him! He got rapist blood in him; he might grow up to be a rapist!" he said while staggering away.

My chest felt like it was about to cave in. I couldn't believe he said some shit like that about my son. Why did I love him so much?

It' going to be ok. I thought to myself.

We can go to the store fast and I will just give him some Tylenol to make him sleep so he won't get into anything.

Armed with a plan I jumped up quickly and went into the kid's room.

"You ok, Mommy?" Wayne asked me sadly, while holding his little sister in his arms. Their tv played cartoons and she was completely into it, Wayne had tears rolling down his face. I knew he heard us fighting. I wiped his face and kissed him on the forehead.

"Yes baby, mommy is good." I said to him smiling, while grabbing my small baby out of her bassinette. I laid her onto the bed and went to grab my other daughter, to put her on some pants. After putting her on pants, I went into the medicine cabinet and grabbed the children's Tylenol.

"Come here, Wayne."

He walked over to me as I was unscrewing the white top.

"BITCH HURRY UP, THAT'S WHY I WANTED TO LEAVE THEY ASS!" I heard Mason screaming from downstairs.

"Yes, Ma."

"Open mouth, I need you to take some of this." I told him.

"But, Ma I ain't sick." he said.

"Boy, do what I told you!" I told him aggravated.

He opened his mouth and swallowed the Tylenol. He walked to the closet to get his shoes, but I called him back.

"Baby, I need you to stay home for mama, ok."

"I don't want to stay with him; he mean!" my son said as the tears welled up in his eyes.

"I know, I know. He won't be here, ok. Just you, my big boy. I'm taking the girls, so they won't bother you, but my big boy I need you stay here for me."

"Mommy I don't want to stay by myself, the monsters might get me! Please don't make me! I won't say nothing I'll be really good." he said heading back towards the closet to grab his shoes. I could no longer hold the tears back as they streamed down my face.

"Wayne please, I need you to please do this." I cried out to him.

He looked at me and bit his bottom lip, like he did when he was thinking about something deeply.

"Ok, mommy, be careful and please come back to me." he said before walking back to his spot in front of the TV.

BUNNNNNKKKKK BUNNNKKKKK!

My Mother's Man

Mason had made it to the car, so he was blowing the horn like crazy. I knew that if I didn't come out, he would come back in to get me and it would be hell to pay, so I grabbed the babies and ran out of the door. I had to leave before I could look back and see my son's face.

∞∞∞

"You dumb as fuck, I said I wanted HOG MAWS not no funky ass chittlings!" Mason said to me as soon as I placed the red bucket of Chitterlings in the grocery cart. I took them out of the cart as fast as I could and reached for the pack of hog Maws.

"It's going to take them things the whole day to cook, Net!" he said before turning his attention back to his daughter.

"Don't grow up to be like your mah mah, she slow. Yes she is, yes she is, daddy baby smart like daddy!" he said in his baby voice as he played with our two year old. She laughed and giggled at his silly faces.

"Grab the stuff and hurry up, we going to the front. I'm tired of walking." he said. I hadn't respond as fast as he liked, so he moved closer to me and yelled loudly in my ear "EARTH TO NET, NET, NET!" and started laughing as he walked away. My stomach churned.

Lord please, please, please let my baby be ok. Watch over him Jesus. I prayed to myself when I heard a woman's voice on the side of me.

"You know if you put up with that, it will continue to get worse." she said to me without looking in my direction but picking through the large batches of Collard Greens.

"It's nothing like that, he's just silly." I said trying to do damage control, not wanting this nosey woman to call the cops.

"Yeah he's silly and he's the only one laughing." she said "But look, I know the signs. I was in an abusive relationship with my ex-husband and the father of my son for 15 years. I can help you if you

63

let me."

I turned to face her.

"Turn back around and look at the vegetables baby." she said, "keep your back to the isle, if he notices you talking to me and not getting the groceries, he will go off."

I turned back to face the vegetables.

"You don't understand, ma'am. I have a 3rd grade education, I can't read or write, I don't have any family that supports me, I live with him and he takes care of me and my children; I can't just leave." I told her while picking up an onion and turning it over as if I was inspecting the quality of it.

"Do you work? "she asked me while putting down a bunch of Collard Greens and picking up a bunch of turnips. "The sooner you start making your own money, the sooner you can build something for you and your babies without him."

I thought back to my son at home alone; A four-year-old in a huge house alone and terrified. I didn't understand why Mason wanted to bully my baby. I would be his punching bag all day, but my baby didn't have anything to do with nothing. Tears filled my eyes and I quickly wiped them away with the back of my hand.

"I don't have any skills." I told her sadly.

"Well I manage housekeeping at a hotel. If you can't do anything else, I know you can cook and clean." she said.

"Yes, I can clean."

"Good, here is my business card." she said placing the card on top of the vegetables. "Cook for him, clean, and make him really happy tonight. Tell him that you know he's under a lot of pressure taking care of you and the kids and you are ready to pull your weight. Tell him that you overheard one of the ladies in the grocery store talking about The Plaza Hotel in Midtown and how they need people to clean up bad. Tell him it won't interfere with your housework or taking care of the kids, you just love him and want to take some pressure *off him.*" she said.

"It may not work," I said hanging my head.

"Try baby, just try. Tell him you will give him your whole paycheck for the bills. You can start off giving him the first few checks. I can give you a raise and pay you the difference under the table."

"Whatever he does to you for asking, can't be any worse than what he has already done to you." she said turning to walk away.

"BRING YOUR SLOW ASS ON, HOW LONG DOES IT TAKE TO PICK SOME VEGETABLES?!" Mason screamed from the back of the store.

I was so embarrassed. People were stopping and looking in his direction, trying to see who he was yelling at. I didn't want to acknowledge him because of the embarrassment but I knew if I pretended that he wasn't talking to me, he would come back up the isle and make a scene. An image flashed in my head of him dragging me by my hair out of the store and people laughing. I didn't want that fantasy to become a reality, so I spoke up.

"I'm... I'm. Coming, baby." I said to him while grabbing the onion, bell pepper, and carrots for the pot roast.

"Don't forget the greens!" he said to me while turning and walking towards the register.

I turned around and picked up the greens with the woman's business card on top of it. Quickly putting the card in my back pocket, I rushed to the front of the store.

"I appreciate you so much, Ms. Arlene." I told my boss after my celebration party ended and the staff returned to work.

"No problem, baby. I called the phone the other day and it said it was disconnected. Is Mason still paying the bills? Did you need my help with anything?" she asked me with a concern look.

"No, he is not paying the bills. He hasn't come home in weeks and nothing has been paid. I'm fine though by the grace of

God. The only thing that has been turned off is the phone." I lied. I didn't want her to offer me money. I would work and get paid the next week and make a way for me and my 3 children.

"Well, I can't say that I'm terribly upset that he hasn't come home; you have needed time to heal from the mess that he caused. You wouldn't have been able to heal with him adding fresh bruises and injuries to the ones you have." she said. "Your next step is to move from that house. You don't owe him to keep his bills afloat in *his* house, that he can come and put you out of at any time. This is the time to save your checks and find a nice place for you and the kids to go. I even spoke with HR, and since you are a regular full-time employee, I got them to add some leave pay on to your check. Leave that house just like his behind did. Don't wait there like a sitting duck!" she warned me while shaking her finger.

"Ms. Arlene, I love that house and it's the only house my children know. I'm not picking up and moving my kids for no reason. Besides, maybe when Mason comes home and realizes how good I have been handling everything without him, he'll realize that I am good for him and change his ways. I have been praying for him, you told me to pray for him." I told her shaking my finger back at her.

"Child, you will learn one day. I just pray it's not too late." she said walking away. "Oh yeah, I changed your assignment from housekeeping to laundry. I don't want you to do anything too heavy too soon. So, just take it easy so we can keep you." she said smiling and walking away.

My heart smiled. It was little moments like that, with people like her, that showed me that God hadn't given up on me yet.

Chapter Nine
<u>Mason</u>

"Damn, what you are talking about, where is your manager?! Let me see your manager, ole Einstein looking motherfucker!" I said to the banker angrily, while standing over the man's desk. As a business owner, I knew how to get on any one's level and speak professionally, but my blood was boiling at the thought of losing a house that was bought and paid for with my hard-earned money, behind some funky ass property taxes.

That dumb hoe Net wasn't good for nothing. Yes, the property taxes were already behind but if she could read, she would have noticed the bank saying that the house was being foreclosed. At that moment she could have gone and done whatever it was she needed to do to get some money to delay the process until I returned. So here I was being the angry black man the media portrayed me to be, so I could get some damn results.

While sorting through the mail to look at the notices to see how much the disconnected bills were, I ran across notices from Navy Federal Credit Union. They couldn't be good, because they were sent on brightly colored paper. In my experience I knew anything sent on brightly colored paper meant bad news.

She done let the whole house go to shit while I was gone?! I thought to myself as I opened the first notice.

NOTICE OF FORECLOSURE

Was the first line I noticed in big bold letters at the top of the page.

"They got me fucked up!" I said to myself aloud as I skimmed down the page.

So, I go honeymoon with my new wife in Aruba and her ass let my house get foreclosed! I thought to myself in disbelief as I opened notice after notice, asking for the homeowner to make contact to work out a payment arrangement for the property taxes.

Maybe they could still work out something with me, I thought. I wasn't ready to give up my side pussy pad just yet. I quickly headed upstairs so I could get changed and catch the bank before it closed, when my clumsy ass fell face down. My brother always got on me about forgetting to look down. I told him it wasn't shit for me down there, so it wasn't no reason for me to train my vision on something that wasn't beneficial.

"SHIT!!" I screamed from the ground as I rubbed my ankle.

I had been in this house enough years to know every step, nook, and cranny, so something was clearly out of place. I began to feel around to see what tripped me, when my hand landed on a big, orange industrial outdoor extension cord. *What the hell* I thought to myself. When I attempted to pick it up, wires pulled it back down. Finding it strange I followed the wires through the house and out the back door, getting madder and madder with each step. *Leave it to her to do some ghetto shit like this!*

When the wire led me all the way to the neighbor's back door, it continued to the inside of the house. I didn't mess around with these people, so I began to knock on the door to get some answers. I tried to keep my cool and knock politely, but feeling like they were trying to test me, I began to bang on the door.

BAM.BAM.BAM!

"STOP BANGING ON MY DAMN DOOR!" The snobby traitor

bitch answered angrily with two crying babies in her arms.

"Why the hell do you have a cord running from your house to mine?" I asked her.

I tried to be polite, but I wasn't sure how it came out because I never did like her or her cracker husband. Out of all the black men she could have chosen, she wanted to go get a white boy. It was always the pretty, sophisticated, black sisters, that wanted the white boys. I had gotten my own revenge though; with this pretty heiress I'd just bagged.

"Well, I was helping out your woman because she didn't have power. I've been keeping the kids for her too. I have them now; do you want to take them home?" she asked me while trying to hand me a screaming, swaddled Bonnie.

It was too soon for me and if she had the kids all this time, she could keep their little asses until Netta came home. I took a step back.

"I didn't bring them here, so I am not taking them anywhere. Did you open my mail too? With your helping, nosey ass! You had to do it, cause she damn sho can't read!" I said asking her the question then answering before she got the chance to.

"Look, I'm not her, so what you can do is get the fuck away from my doorstep before I get my husband out here to bust a cap in your black ass!" she said while turning her back on me and slamming the door in my face with her foot.

She made it a few steps away, when she heard the sound of the brick going through her back window. The flying glass caused her to drop to her knees and lean over to protect the crying babies.

"YOU BLACK TOO, BITCH! I GUESS YOU FORGOT CAUSE THAT OLD ASS WHITE MAN AINT TAMEING YOU RIGHT, YOU DON'T TALK TO NO REAL MAN LIKE THAT!" I said while walking away triumphantly, back next door.

Tracy

It angered me to think about what would have happened if I wasn't walking away so quickly; the brick could have hit my baby in the damn head. Mason didn't care if I or either one of the babies in my arms were injured. It was exactly why I never dealt with black men; they were lazy, controlling, spoiled and selfish. My mother had taught me at a young age that white men were better, and they knew how to take good care of their women. Since I was old enough to date, I'd never dated a man of my own race.

My husband heard the glass shattering and, came flying down the stairs.

"What in the world? Are you ok? Are the kids ok?" he asked while grabbing one of the screaming babies from my arms to help. He'd came in to take a quick nap before he had to head back to the office, so I'd stayed downstairs to keep the crying from disturbing him.

"Yeah, that hood rat next door busted our damn window!" I said in disbelief.

"I thought she was at work. Why would she do that?" he asked confused.

"No, no it was the man that lives there, not her. I haven't seen him in a while but, I guess he is back now. I asked him did he want to take the kids home, he gets smart. He starts ranting about me reading his notices she asked me to read."

"Oh Really? How about I head over there and have a talk with that young punk. I told you to stay out of their business baby, bu, no you have to be little Ms. Helpful!" My husband said while walking towards the door.

"NO! NO! TOM, DON'T!" I said while grabbing him back with my free hand. "It's not even worth it. His broke ass hasn't been paying the taxes on that house, it's been foreclosed and sold. They have one week left before the Marshal's evict them. Jeanette can't read, she has been having me read all the notices. I didn't even tell her about the foreclosure because I want him gone! I can't stand his ghetto, loud color wearing behind! They are about to get tossed out on their asses!" I said trying to calm my husband down.

My husband had too much to lose and I would be damned if I would let him go out there and get in some trouble, for whipping some young punk's ass. I could get on the phone, and get the window replaced in an hour. I felt guilty for not being honest with Jeanette which was the only reason I was being so helpful, allowing her to use our electricity, and keeping an eye on her kids for her while she went to work her little job. I didn't have anything against the young woman and the kids, it was that disrespectful punk that I wanted the hell out of the neighborhood.

Mason

Mr. Mason Vactor you haven't paid property taxes on the property in five years" the man said stuttering and, pushing his bifocal eyeglasses closer to his eyes with the tip of his index finger. "My records show that for the past few months, we have tried to call the telephone number on file which was disconnected. We also sent out around 20 notices, multiple notices a week, to get you to come into the bank and pay any amount that you could afford to continue to own and live in your house. We didn't receive any communication from you, we didn't receive any funds from you; the property taxes were paid, and the house was bought. You were given 30 days to vacate the premises or the Henry County Marshal's office will come and evict your things; you have one week to leave the premises before that happens. Didn't you receive the notices, sir?" The man asked in confusion.

"Who the hell is over you? You can't be too high up the management chain because if you did, your ass would be on a beach somewhere, you wouldn't be in here working!" I replied snidely. "Corporate, give me the number to corporate!" I said to him not giving a damn about the nosey people standing around looking. I loved the attention, and as soon as the sisters got a good look at me, I was guaranteed to walk out of here with one of them for a few hours of fun. They couldn't resist me.

"Sir, that is enough!" said the armed guard as he walked toward me interrupting my shine time. His partner followed closely behind with his hand on his pistol.

"Enough of what? I'm just having a conversation with this man." I said while flexing my muscles and putting on a good show.

"Please, remove him from the premises." the banker said, while taking a hard swallow and pointing at me like a scared child. He looked around at all the people watching the commotion unfold, he was glad that the armed security guards finally decided to step in and do something.

"Ok, I see what's going on. Y'all trying to railroad me because I'm a strong, successful, black brother." I said while nodding my head and backing out of the man's face.

I was cocky but I wasn't stupid. I couldn't get no ass with bullet holes in my body, so I chose to let them win. I would miss my Pussy Pad but I could just let my new thang buy me another house; an even bigger one. I didn't know what Net and the kids was going to do but, it was her own damn fault for being illiterate. I grabbed the notices off the table.

"All I want is the number to corporate, can you tell him to give me that?" I asked pointing in his direction, mockingly.

"Here, hand him this pamphlet the number is on the back." the bank manager said while thrusting the pamphlet into the guard's hands. "Please remove him now"

I turned to walk away with my head held high, opening my silk shirt a little more to let my sexy chest hairs show through.

"YALL AINT GOT NO RESPECT FOR THE BLACK MAN! MARTIN LUTHER KING, BROTHER MALCOLM, NONE OF EM MEAN NOTHING TO Y'ALL! WE STILL AINT GOT NO DAMN RIGHTS!" I yelled while walking out of the bank's doors, causing an even bigger scene.

I held my closed fist in the air to symbolize black power. All the sisters loved the black men that wasn't scared to stand up to, *the man,* it got their pussy wetter than a swimming pool. I saw a few sisters inside looking at me and smiling like they wanted me to keep preaching the gospel. One in particular, stood out to me. A caramel colored thing, she was about Net's height. She wore a cropped top and some bell bottom jeans, tight enough to show that fat monkey print. What I liked the most about her body was those baby making hips on her.

I nodded my head at her and licked my lips. She stepped out of the teller line to walk towards me, grateful to be the chosen one. I would bend her over my car seat and have a little fun before I headed back to the house, to give Net a goodbye ass kicking. I also needed to pack the few things I wanted to keep, before the Marshal's came next week to toss everything else out.

My new wife would replace my work van, art, and everything else I wanted and needed; because I was a bad motherfucker like that.

Chapter Ten
Netta

When I got off the bus, I was tired, sore, and starving but It felt good to accomplish something that I knew would help me and my children. I stopped by the neighbor's house to grab my little munchkins. Tracy lived in the house closest to mine with her husband and adopted, 6-month-old daughter Rose. She was a little younger than my mother and looked to be in her early 30's. She was always pretty; I knew that had to be because of that white man she was married to taking good care of her. I never saw her go to or come from nobody's job, so I knew she had to be a stay home wife and mother.

"Thank you so much for keeping my brats for me." I told her when she gave me my youngest daughter's baby bag. "Did they give you a hard time?" I asked her, trying to start conversation.

"No, they were ok, but your piece of shit baby's father needs an attitude adjustment and I unplugged your extension cord!" she said going into her house and shutting the door in my face.

I stood on her porch with my daughter's carrier in the crook of my arm, her baby bag hanging from my shoulder, and my son and daughter each holding one of my hands. My eyes filled with tears. Every time I tried to take a few steps forward, it seemed as if I was knocked five steps back. How was I supposed to warm up my daughter's milk or warm up some soup for my children for dinner with no electricity? I turned to walk across the lawn to the house. After letting go of my child's hand and putting the carrier at my feet, I went into my purse to retrieve the key and open the door. When I made it inside of the house, there sitting on the couch shirtless with a bottle of Evian in hand, was Mason.

The first emotion I felt was surprise; anger followed closely behind. It had been months since he'd just up and left me to fiend for this huge household, as well as his two daughters. I understood that I was expected to be Wayne's mother and father, but Terri and Bonnie had a woman beating, money taking, piece of shit father, live and in the flesh. Who the hell was he to decide that he just needed to take a break?!

"Glad you decided to come back around." I said, while bringing the kids inside to get settled; placing my daughter's carrier on the couch.

As soon as I turned around, I was met by his fist.

"You are a poor ass excuse for a woman, do you get that?!" he asked while standing over me. "I'm gone a few weeks, A FEW DAMN WEEKS, and you can't even keep the household up! You ain't good for shit but laying on your back and having babies; out here begging people for electricity!" he said, while kicking me in my side with his alligator, pointy toed, shoe. I winced in pain as his shoe connected to my side. Once, twice, then a third time.

"Bitch next door and her uppity husband don't like me, and you give them a reason to laugh at me?! Got them powering my house, reading my notices, feeding my baby daughter, and all in my business! Why haven't you paid the bills? You work, what you been doing with the money all this time, huh? You getting high like ya mama? You giving another nigga all your money?" he asked before punching me in the face, causing my head to fall back and hit the couch cushion.

"I haven't been taking drugs, and I haven't been with another man. I haven't been to work, the doctor put me on bedrest because my ribs were cracked. They wouldn't let me go back to work until I healed. To... Today was my first day back to work" I said stuttering trying to get the explanation out as quickly as my mouth could form the words.

My toddler daughter stood in the same spot I left her in, she had begun to cry and was wiping her eyes with the back of her small hand. My son rushed over to her and tried to pick her up, even though she was almost as big as he was. Giving up on picking her up, he pulled her into the corner and began to rub her back.

"What your lil rapist ass doing?!" Mason yelled out to him startling him, causing him to jump. He immediately stopped consoling his little sister and put his face into his hands.

"Good. Keep your hands off her you lil rapist!" he said to Wayne before turning his attention back on me.

"So, what the hell happened to your ribs?" he asked while sitting back on the couch and picking up his bottled of water to take a sip.

"I... I got jumped on by some girls, when I went to take the pictures with the kids." I said to him while wiping the tears from my face; grateful that the beating was over for now.

"What you do for them to jump you, you out here starting shit?" he asked before wiping the sweat from his chocolate face, with the back of his large hand.

"No. The girl said she gave you clap and you told her you couldn't deal with her no more because your ole lady made you choose between the women in the streets or her." I said to him without looking him in the eye.

He began to laugh.

"Damn, I can't believe she went for that shit. I really was just tired of her ass. Just so you know though, this is on you, ok. This is all your damn fault!" he said standing up and walking towards the stairs.

"Please don't go, Mason. I'll do anything" I yelled out to him hoping that he was just going upstairs to change into something more comfortable so we could sit down and talk things through. My anger was replaced with happiness because he had finally come home. I knew that he would come back home to me and the kids eventually. I was glad that I hadn't left like Ms. Arlene suggested because he wouldn't have known where to find me. I was sure that It would have killed him to come home to an empty house without his family.

It had taken him longer upstairs than I expected but, it was his first day home, so I didn't want to nag him. I hoped that he would come downstairs soon and help me come up with a plan to feed the kids because I was sure they were hungry. What I expected wasn't what I received when I noticed him walking down the stairs with two large suitcases in each hand, and his hat tilted. I didn't understand where he was going. He had only been home for about an hour.

"What are you doing? Where are you going? Please don't go I can fix this! I get paid next week, if you go and pay the bills and get some groceries you can take my check. I can fix you something really good to eat and do my hair!"

"You know what, Net, you ain't good for shit!" he said, angrily. "All you know how to do is house shit, and you barley know how to please me right! I'm out, you can have this house for you and the kids cause I ain't going to leave y'all outside, but me and your thang is through!" he told me, trying to walk away before I grabbed him.

"Mayday, please baby! You told me you would never leave, we matched blood!" I told him, reminding him by holding up my scarred finger.

One night we were drunk and we both cut the tips of our index fingers and touched them together. Mason told me that it was how people got married in Africa. He told me they called it, *matching blood*, and it meant that we were bonded to each other for life. When we matched blood, I knew that I would always belong to him and he would always belong to me.

"Look, yeah we did but all this is too much; these kids getting on my nerves and so are you. It just aint no happiness here for me, so dammit let me go!"

"NO, I WON'T LET YOU GO! I'LL KILL MYSELF; I'LL KILL THESE KIDS! I'm not letting you go!", I told him hoping that if he didn't have a heart for me, he at least had a heart for his two little girls since I had threatened their lives.

My lip was busted from his punches, I had dried blood under my nostril from my bloody nose. My uniform pants were stained red from the blood I wiped from my nose, and my hair was a tangled nappy mess. Mason looked at me as if he knew that I would probably do it if he left me in that condition, so he dropped his suitcases.

"Ok, Alright! Just know that I will leave your ass anytime, don't take me for a joke!" he said, while walking up the stairs because he knew I would collect the suitcases and bring them up behind him.

"I don't baby, I don't" I said relieved that I had convinced him to stay and starting to smile. I began to grab his suitcases so I could take them upstairs and put his things away.

"Hurry up with those suitcases so I can tap that ass before I go pay these bills!" he told me.

I began walking faster, almost tripping over my feet, as the heavy suitcases felt like they were about to rip my arms from their sockets. I didn't care that my newborn had started to cry and was probably hungry, as long as my man wasn't going anywhere.

When I woke up from our backbreaking love making session and reached for Mason, I felt an empty spot where he had once been. Every hole on my body was sore because I had given him my all, letting him have me any way he wanted me.

I wanted to show my appreciation for the fact that he didn't leave. I figured he had probably gone to the bathroom, so I tried to get up and check on him. As if an invisible force was holding me down, my attempts to stand were unsuccessful. I'd heard of this before; we called it the witch riding us down south when we were unable to move certain parts of our body. If the witch was riding you, you were probably still sleeping.

Maybe I was dreaming that he wasn't there so, I allowed myself to relax, then blacked out as if I had been sprinkled with the most powerful sleeping dust known to man.

Chapter Eleven
<u>Mason</u>

♪Come here, mama
And dig this crazy scene
He's not too fancy
But his line is pretty clean
He ain't no drag
Papa's got a brand new bag
He's doing The Jerk
He's doing The Fly
Don't play him cheap
'Cause you know he ain't shy♪

"I know I owe Lucci but see, I'm rich baby!! My wife over there ain't no regular snow bunny; that there is Layla Hitman, daughter of Patrick Hitman. He owns Hitman Hotels and she is an heiress! Lucci knows all this. That hundred K I owe is pennies compared to what we have!"

I said before Layla screamed out, "HUNDRED K? WHAT THE HELL DO YOU MEAN HUNDRED K?!"

I looked at her and shook my head while waving my hand. "I got this honey bun, ok just keep quiet."

"KEEP QUIET MY ASS! YOU'RE NOT THE ONE GETTING BEATEN AND RAPED!" She screamed at me while crying out loud.

The henchman looked back and forth between us like they were watching a ping pong match, as if we had time to argue back and forth. I tried to explain to Layla that these men were in our house at 2am because I owed their boss, Lucci, 100 thousand dollars.

WHAACCCK!!

One of the men slapped Layla, she fell from her knees to her side. I didn't flinch, it was better her than me.

"Silence all this shit, if you didn't know now you do. Your husband owes a powerful man a lot of money, sweet tits. He made some promises that's going to cost him an arm and a leg if he doesn't pay up!" The Italian man said, while standing over a whimpering Layla.

"Ok listen," I said. "like I was saying before she cut me off, that hundred k is pennies compared to what her father has! Tell Lucci I will have his money for him first thing in the morning, I swear it!" I told the men braver than I felt.

Truthfully, I didn't know what was about to happen, but I prayed whatever they did, they just did it to Layla as a warning to me. I was more concerned about my own life than the life of my wife. I was glad that they didn't have any funny business going on and were only interested in raping her; I'd heard stories of them tough acting jokers swinging both ways.

"Please, please, I didn't know anything about this honest to God!" Layla said crying while holding the side of her face. "Anything I ask my father for, he'll give it. Just please give us until tomorrow to pay his debt!" Her lips were swollen and bloody, she looked filthy.

Her bleached blonde hair was lifeless, and limp weighed down by dirt, sweat, spit, and the semen the men had spewed all over her, when they were done with her. She now regretted the fact that she'd spent so much time and money to make herself look as perfect as her mother did, because the men couldn't keep their grimy hands off of her. The constant groping and fingers put in any place they wanted at random times, made her wish they would just kill her so the nightmare would end. If she made it out alive, truthfully, the men wouldn't see a penny of her daddy's money; she was completely humiliated.

The four men had taken turns beating and raping her and all she could think about was how her piece of shit new husband had gotten her into this shit. There was no denying at this point that she should have listened to her father.

I reminisced on the day we met as I watched the men beat

My Mother's Man

her like she was useless trash on the sidewalk instead of the daughter of one of the wealthiest men in the world.

I had been her first piece of good, black dick, so when I'd proposed to her after 4 months of dating, she said yes impulsively. Her father, the owner of over 40 Hitman Hotels and a real estate tycoon, advised against it. Layla Hitman was his only daughter and his pride and joy. She was the epitome of privilege. Her perfect face, matched her perfect body, matched her perfect house, her perfect car, and her perfect wardrobe. Which all made her life a perfect bore. So, when she met me at a house party while she was out with some friends, she knew that I was heaven sent. She reminded me of my ex-wife Maria. Beautiful and naïve. It was funny how fathers spoiled their daughters but, didn't give them the tools they needed to be able to see through and run from niggas like me. Then they chose to not like me because I used their weaknesses to my advantage.

I was sexy and Lacey could see this large dick through my tight jeans. I saw the wheels turning in her mind and lust was written all over her face. With her being a snow bunny I was sure that fucking with me would piss off some Clan mask wearing nigga so I knew I would have to get in, get what I wanted from her quickly, and get out smoothly. After watching her watch me all night, I walked over to her and offered to get her something to drink. She accepted and within 5 minutes started to complain about her rich daddy. She was making this too easy. She told me I was charming and a great listener; Unlike her father I didn't cut her off when she spoke more than 3 words. So, after shouting over the music for 45 minutes, I invited her to go Winn Park, which was only a few blocks away; she obliged. The park had trails for joggers and a really nice pond. At that time of night, it was completely deserted, and we had it all to ourselves.

We drunk beer and snorted lines of cocaine while talking about our lives. The drugs and alcohol made her spill her guts to me as if I were Jackie; her therapist her father paid to figure out why she was so unhappy with the amazing life he'd given her.

"See, from what you telling me is, your old man just don't respect you as a woman you know and, your mama don't care either way, as long as she can shop and keep her fancy lifestyle." I told her as I snorted the line off her leg before throwing my head back onto her lap. I pinched the bridge of my nose to absorb every piece of the substance while I waited for it to take me on a wild ride.

"I agree!!!! You have only known me two hours and you get me more than my parents do. He thinks a shopping spree, a car or a vacation will fix anything. I hate having money and access to anything I want; I'm bored out of my mind and I don't cherish any of it because I know it's all replaceable at the snap of my fingers!" she told me. Sensing that her high was coming down, I sat up and sprinkled some of the powder on my forearm and held it out to her, so she could do a line.

"Hell, I know you more than them because I respect you. You a full-grown woman that know what she wants and needs. Most girls your age, don't know anything; you smarter than all of them. You so beautiful and mature, I'm falling for you and I haven't even known you a full day!" I said to her while rubbing my fingers through her hair, when she lowered her head.

After her long sniff, she shook her head from side to side as my words mixed with the drugs. I had her emotions on a roller coaster ride, and she didn't want to get off.

"So, if I'm beautiful why haven't you tried to fuck me yet?" she asked while chewing on her bottom lip.

"Cause you not like the rest of these thrown away girls, I care for you even though we just met."

She looked me in my big brown eyes and felt that my words were sincere. She leaned over and kissed me with all the passion in her petite, body. It was like the kiss was my green light, because I grabbed her by her hair and pulled her head back, to deepen the kiss and show her who was in control. Giggling she confirmed what I'd already knew. I stood up from the park bench, continuing to hold her by her hair. I knew exactly what she needed. I didn't know why a bitch with a daddy, had daddy issues but clearly, she needed someone to take control of her ass and I was the man for the job.

Glad that the park was empty I took her over to the tire swing and bent her over it. Flipping up her short, white dress to reveal some sexy satin panties, I cupped her pussy and began to squeeze, while grinding on her ass.

"MMMMHM!" she moaned, as her juices caused her thin panties to moisten.

I moved the satin panties that probably cost more than my shoes to the side, and rubbed my hands over her bald, woman hood.

I loved women that maintained themselves and kept their lawns manicured; I had been with all types. The extra prissy women that spent hundreds of dollars on waxes, and grooming; as well as the dumpster bitches, that half washed their asses like they were in middle school. It was ironic to me that this heiress, rich bitch was bent over taking the same dick that went to broke, ghetto, welfare check getting Tasha, less than 24 hours ago. She wouldn't wear the same cheap draws Tasha wore but, here she was bouncing on the same pole.

"THIS BIG, BLACK, DICK GOOD AINT IT?! AINT THIS DICK BETTER THAN THAT LIL PINK SASUAGE THEM WHITE BOYS THROWING!" *I said to her aggressively, slamming into her so hard the skin on her ass turned bright red.*

I held the tire swing by its long ropes to keep her in place and punished her for all her ancestors who'd done it to my ancestors. When her pussy began to grip me tighter, I knew what was about to go down; it was time to act an ass. I flipped her on her back then turned her upside down, like I was Popeye the Sailor, steering the ship. Her head was now where her legs once were, I gripped each leg instead of the ropes of the tire swing. I fucked her like it was the last piece of ass I would ever have. After that day we were inseparable. She told me to hire help instead of going to work. Even though my brother didn't take too kindly to it, It was my good dicking that got us the company so he knew to keep his jealous mouth shut.

We spent our days holed up in her Buckhead loft, snorting lines, drinking, and smoking; before the gambling started.

"Hey, stop all that damn daydreaming!" the man yelled at me snapping his fingers in front of my face. "You don't get to zone out, watch what we do to your wife because this is your own damn fault!" he said to me while unzipping his hands and peeing on her.

Actually it's her fault, I thought to myself as I thought about how I met Lucci to borrow the money. It was her own stinginess that got her into this position.

It was her idea to go to Las Vegas because she hadn't been in a while and she wanted to "show me something different" were her exact words. She was sure that I was head over heels in love with her because there was nothing that she wouldn't give me. I'd always tell her that she was the best woman I'd ever had, and she believed me.

She took me to Vegas, and we stayed in Caesar's Palace. The beautiful hotel and casino had me practically salivating at the mouth and, when I'd won 1,000 dollars the first night, she knew that mini trip would go down in the history books.

When we returned home a week later, my spirits were in the dumps because every penny I'd won, I'd lost. She tried to convince me that it was all in the name of fun, but I was a sore loser. I wanted to get right back on the plane and go back to try again. She told me no and figured I would get over it. She figured wrong! I wouldn't sleep with her; I would leave before she woke up and come back after she went to sleep, leaving little things out of place so she would know that I'd been home. I could hold the hell out of a grudge, and I held that grudge for an entire week.

Missing my affection and love making, she booked the trip for us to go back. When I came into the house later that evening expecting her to be in bed, she was wide awake; our bags were packed, and she was sipping a mimosa from a champagne flute and smoking a joint. When I noticed our packed bags, I knew my little silent treatment worked. I made sure to thank her for her change of heart, all night long.

When we returned to Vegas, gone was the innocence and fun; the vibe was replaced with awkward undertones. It felt more like a business trip than a vacation to Layla. She prayed that I would take the 10,000 dollars she'd given me and not lose it all but win the few thousand I had lost to readjust my ego. Her prayers went unanswered when I lost the 10,000 dollars and stumbled pissy drunk to our suite, demanding that she give me more because I was, so close to winning big!

At that point the entire trip had cost her more than it was worth, so it was her turn to be spoiled and demand her way. It worked on her daddy so she was sure it would work on me.

"Look we married now, so what's yours ain't just yours no more its ou-. Ours!" I stuttered while swaying back and forth, barely able to keep my balance.

"I know that Mayday, I'm not an idiot. I just don't think this is a good business move to spend more and-"

"What the hell do you know about business?!" I asked her while still swaying.

"Your father is the businessman, not you! You were just lucky enough to come out of the right nut sack, you don't know a damn thing about business! I have my own business; I know smart business moves. I see what it is, you just don't want me to hit it big because you like feeling like you have more money than me; that's what this is?" I said.

"No, I don't care about the money it's ours, you know that!" she said sitting up on the bed.

"Well, do you know how it makes me feel that I can't buy you the things you used to, Layla? I love you more than my life; I want to spoil you like your daddy does! My business has always been enough for me until I met you. I'm not making money for just me no more, I'm making money for us now! I want us to have a family; I want kids, I'm ready to be a father. I can't provide for them on the scale that they would be used to, making what I make now. Just please give me 10,000 more dollars and I will make this shit happen!" I said while rubbing her face softly.

"I can't do that." She replied.

My face twisted up; an expression crossed my face that she had never seen before. Just as quickly as it came it was gone and I smiled. "Ok sweets." I said. "I'm going to get some fresh air, be right back."

She didn't want me to leave, but she knew I needed some space, so she let me go.

The next day when she woke up, our suitcases were filled and sitting upright next to the bed. She stretched and turned over to find a note on the bedside table, underneath the lamp.

Went to grab some breakfast for us, I changed our flight schedule to head home today. They didn't have a problem because of the first class; they just made sure to let me know that they would charge the account on file for the ticket difference because of the day change. You were right, I was being ridiculous spending money for our future on fantasies.

Love,
Your Husband

Her heart fluttered; aside from the sex, this was why she fell for me and accepted my proposal after only four months. I was so sweet, and I knew how to admit to the things I did wrong and my mistakes.

She wished her father could do the same. When he was wrong, he just threw her a credit card and told her to have fun. It didn't matter to him that the words, I'm sorry, would mean more to her than a Chanel purse.

Her eyes filled with tears and, she got out of the big fluffy bed that felt almost as good as her bed at home; Almost. She went to the bathroom and looked to see that I had packed up everything except her toiletries that she would need to freshen up before they left. I'd left out her toothbrush, expensive face cream, her La Perla matching underwear set, her Gucci animal print wrap dress and her black knee Gucci boots. Her jewelry was laid out in the exact combination she would wear it, which let her know that I really did pay attention to the details about her. Her mother and father were married after years of dating and it didn't make their marriage any better, so she didn't care that we'd married fast. I knew her inside out and clearly, I loved her deeply.

Layla curled into a fetal position and cried softly. She prayed to God that he would send her parents her love from the afterlife if she didn't make it to see tomorrow, because she now knew that they were the only ones that cared about her. She realized that instead of defying her father she should have cherished him, because he was a good man. He had his flaws like men did and he was tough on her, but he truly loved her.

The love she thought she had was nothing compared to her parent's love. Even if they did fight sometimes, she knew for a fact that her father would have never allowed men to do to her mother what I was allowing to happen, without so much as any piece of emotion. I hadn't shed a tear or tried to fight to fight for her. Hell, I hadn't even told the men to stop while she screamed for me to help her, as they violated her repeatedly. It was as if I cared more about what they would do to me if he stood up for her, than I cared about what they were doing. I'd gladly used her name to prove that I had the means to repay the debt though. She realized now what her father had been saying all along; I was only using her for her name and money. I didn't genuinely love her like I'd told her when I was drunk; I just felt that she was lucky enough to come out of the right nut-sack.

This wasn't our first rodeo, so the four henchmen purposely violated my wife in my face to hurt me. When they focused their energy on wives and daughters, it made the toughest men fold. This case was the exact opposite, which was rare, but it did happen, and they knew the protocol in the situation, so they did exactly what Lucky Lucci would order them to do if he were there. They left my woman balled up on the floor and walked over to me.

"NOW, FELLAS LET'S PLAY THIS COOL!" I said when I noticed the shift in focus. Three of the four men were headed in my direction, and one of the men was headed to a big black duffle bag.

"WHAT THE HELL YOU, GETTING FROM THERE?!" I asked the man while turning my head to look at him, quickly turning my head back to the other three, to see what they were about to do. I turned my head a split second too late and my face met the bottom of a boot. I didn't get a chance to bounce back to my knees, before blows rained down on me from every direction. All I felt was pain. I tried to curl up into a ball so the blows could stop connecting to my pretty, chocolate face. I couldn't pull my next catch out here looking like I'd been in a match with Sugar Ray.

"I don't think so, buddy." the man told me grabbing me to keep me from ducking my head down. The other men continued to beat me and kick me in the face, chest, stomach; my insides felt like they were on fire.

The man that was holding my hair grabbed me around my neck to steady me.

"You borrowed an arm and a leg so we're going to take an arm or a leg this time, and if the money isn't in our hands by this time tomorrow, we will take whatever limb we didn't take the first time?"

"OH, HELL NAW, YALL NIGGAS CRA....." I didn't get out the rest of my statement, before one of the men punched me in my mouth knocking the rest of my sentence down my throat.

"So, which one you wanna give us, huh? Or do you want us to choose? Don't worry, we'll choose. Eeeny, Meeny, Miney," the man started pointing back and forth between both my right arm and my right leg, while the other man walked over with a saw.

I couldn't believe I had gotten myself into this shit, as I'd lost my bowels and shitted all over myself.

"So, you a shitter, huh? You too cool of a cat to be out here shitting your pants!" the spokesman said. The other three men remained quiet not saying a word, so I assumed this was their leader.

"Look man, tell em not to do this, ok! Please!" I begged as the man said his final Moe, with his finger landing on my leg.

"Leg it is; hold him down boys!" he said while I thrashed from left to right and tried with all my strength to move. My efforts were useless; they'd come to collect a debt and would continue to collect my body parts until that debt was paid.

Chapter Twelve
<u>Mason</u>

♪ *You keep saying you got something for me*
Something you call love, but confess
You've been messing where you shouldn't have been messing
And now someone else is getting all your best
These boots are made for walking
And that's just what they'll do
One of these days these boots
Are going to walk all over you
You keep lying when you ought to be truthing
You keep losing when you ought to not bet
You keep saming when you ought to be changing
What's right is right, but you ain't been right yet ♪

When I woke up from what must have been a terrible nightmare, I didn't recognize our bedroom. I heard the machines beeping and smelled the over sanitized room, before my eyes opened. Suddenly the scene came rushing back. The Men in masks, The Money I owed Lucci, the raping; taking turns on my screaming wife, turning and beating me, the saw and...

SHIT!

I moved too fast and, my ribs felt like they were separating. I was inside of a hospital. I felt pain from my leg and prayed that it was still there. However, when I looked at the cover's flattened surface where my leg would be, I knew that it was gone.

"AAARGGGHHHHHH, MY LEG! MY FUCKIN LEG! THEY

TOOK MY FUKIN LEG, OH GOD PLEASE, JESUS WHY?" I screamed into the atmosphere while throwing my head back and shaking it from side to side, like a toddler throwing a temper tantrum.

Each dramatic movement caused more pain in my body. I didn't even have to look in a mirror to know I was fucked up; right then I did something I hadn't done since my mother was murdered in front of me, I began to cry. I wept like I'd lost everything in the world because to me, that was the case. My ability to get any woman I wanted, to do whatever it was I wanted them to do, had been my identity since I discovered my gift as a little boy. The little girls I finessed became grown women, and when I became a man, my gift heightened by 1,000. It was the only thing I felt my father truly gave me; even though he had taken so much. Who the hell was going to swoon when I hopped up to them on one leg like a cripple?

"YOU SHOULD HAVE JUST KILLED ME; YOU SHOULD HAVE FUCKIN KILLED ME!" I screamed out loud into the atmosphere when the realization hit me. My heartbeat began to increase rapidly, making the monitors in my room start to go off erratically.

"Mr. Vactor, you have to calm down." One of the nurses said as three other hospital personnel's, rushed in behind her.

"NO, FUCK YOU AND ALL YALL! JUST KILL ME, KILL ME!" I screamed like a maniac as I began to blindly swing in the air. It didn't matter where a hit landed, I just wanted these doctors the fuck up off me.

"I NEED RESTRAINTS AND HALOPERIDOL; 0.5MG IV STAT!" the charge nurse yelled out to her team.

"I'M NOT CRAZY, I'M MAYDAY! I'M MASON! THIS AIN'T ME, I AIN'T CRIPPLE THIS AINT ME!" I screamed before i felt the needle in the crook of my arm.

A warm feeling flooded me like I was under water, and

every muscle in my body relaxed. My head felt too heavy to hold up, so I just let it fall to whichever side it wanted to go. Before everything went dark, I heard one of the men say, "I wonder what happened to the poor bastard."

∞∞∞

When I woke up strapped to a bed, my throat felt too dry to speak and the lights in the room were too bright. I made the best attempt I could make at swallowing, while lowering my eyelids to block some of the light. Sitting in the chair directly next to my bed reading a piece of paper and laughing silently, was the man who had taken my leg. He was the only one in the crew that didn't, have on a mask that night, so I recognized him instantly.

I moved from my back turning to my side, and quickly slid as far to the opposite end of the bed as I could go, without falling on the floor. The sudden movement caused pain to hit me like a ton of bricks as I lowered my forehead to the pillow, to gain control of my pain and emotions.

"Relax bastard, I'm not here to take anything else from you at the moment." the man said in his thick Italian accent.

He had on a brown, golden yellow, and white striped button down shirt and a pair of matching golden yellow slacks; his white loafers completed the outfit and if I hadn't watched him in action, I would have taken the man for one of those wealthy Wall Street Guys, not a heartless henchmen for a mafia boss.

"Wha... Wha... What is it you want? Why didn't you just kill me, huh? Death would have been better than this shit man!"

"Hey. Hey. If you don't calm your ass down, I'll take your fingers and shove them up your ass!" the man said angrily.

I shut my mouth and looked down to the man's feet, where

his black bag sat. It was the bag with the tools. This joker wasn't playing games and I knew it. My mouth found some saliva for a deep gulp and I prayed that a nurse, doctor, janitor, or any damn body would walk through that door.

"Now, I have a flight to catch. I came here to formally let you know that your debt has been paid so your business is done with Lucci. He asked me to send you his love and told me to tell you, that it was a pleasure doing business with you. Also, if you're ever in Vegas again and want to play the craps or do some gambling but you're short on cash, let him know. However," he said while standing. "you now have business with another client of mine, so I came to deliver something to you; see you in 3 days." the man said while laughing and grabbing his black bag to walk out the door.

"3 days? I know I didn't pay it; I'm going to get the money, but I just don't have it right now!" I replied confused.

The man walked back over to the bedside table and grabbed the paperwork he was laughing at and threw it on the bed next to me.

"Read this, it will explain everything. See you in 3 days." he said, while walking out of the door quickly, leaving me to wonder if I imagined the whole scenario.

Picking up the note with a wedding ring I instantly recognized taped to the bottom, and papers stapled to the back of it, I began to read.

My Dearest Mason,

You are the worst thing that ever happened to me, as well as the best. Because of you I was raped, beaten, and humiliated. While I lay on the floor watching you beg for your life and your leg intensely, I realized that not only did you not try to protect me, or beg them not to hurt me, you didn't even ASK them not to. Selfish son of a bitch! However, you are the best thing that ever happened to me because you taught me everything love is not. You also made me value the people who truly love me, the people who I have hurt, and misused the way you used me. I didn't appreciate my family I wanted them to suffer because they gave me a wealthy, amazing life I didn't feel I deserved. I was spoiled and selfish and I only dated you to make them angry. In the end Karma turned out to be a bigger bitch than me and I paid for my mistakes physically, mentally, and financially.

As a thank you for the lessons you taught me, I paid Lucci the hundred grand you owed him. You are now debt free. Also, I attached the wedding ring that your low life ass couldn't afford but since it was the one, I WANTED, I paid for it. You can take it to the pawn shop and get a few hundred dollars for it because that's all they will give you despite its value. This is only because I don't want any reminders that you ever existed. I have attached our divorce papers and, you have 3 days to sign them. I'm glad that you showed me your true colors before I received my 25-million-dollar inheritance on my 21st birthday. Since I was stupid enough to not make you sign a pre-nuptial agreement, you would have received half of my money.

BUT, since right now I'm technically broke and, living off daddy you will get what I "legally have" and that is a big fat NOTHING. If you don't sign the papers in 3 days, let's just say I threw a tip on Lucci's money that will make sure that you go from one leg to no limbs.

Don't have a nice life; have the life you deserve.

-With Hate,

Your Rich Ass Ex-Wife

Chapter Thirteen
PeddleWay

    I responded to a 911 call from a frantic woman stating that her neighbor was really hurt, and lying in a bathtub filled with water. I expected a call like this because usually when the weather was gloomy and around the holidays, I received a lot of suicide calls. The summers in Atlanta were so full of activity. People were at the parks, barbecues, and clubs so they didn't have time to feel depressed. When people were pumped up on adrenaline and fun, I got the car accidents, the violent calls, the rape, and robbery calls. On the flip side of that, when the weather was bad or during the holiday season, people were forced to stay inside and deal with whatever issues they were running away from.

    I had been on the force for a year and a half; still new enough to be affected by certain things but doing it long enough to let a lot of things roll off my back. So, when I arrived at the suburbs in McDonough, Ga, I immediately thought it was probably some spoiled little girl whose parent wouldn't buy her what she wanted, and was probably lashing out for some attention. Or, maybe even a wife whose husband was cheating. What I didn't expect to see was a little boy that looked familiar. When I arrived at the scene, there was a woman standing outside of a beautiful house with one little girl swaddled in a baby pink blanket, and another who was standing next to the woman while she held the little girl's hand, protectively. The little girl looked eerily familiar.

"Officer Peddle Way!" the little boy screamed out while running up to me, grabbing me by my waist.

"Heyy buddy, what's goin on?" I asked him while getting down eye level with the familiar looking child; still not completely placing him.

I had been on a hundred calls with a hundred kids; maybe I had spoken at his school or something. Although I was sure I would have remembered speaking at a school that far out. I usually just spoke at inner city schools; those kids were the ones that were most likely to get tangled into a life of crime and poverty.

"It's my mama, Net." the little boy said as his eyes filled with tears, but they didn't fall, they just brimmed on the surface.

"You took us for ice cream and asked if we was ok at home; I didn't tell the truth we not ok! My mama is really sad." the little boy said, and the events came flooding back. I'd taken the little boy and his little sister for ice cream. Their mother had been in a fight, she was a feisty something and didn't want to go to the hospital. I had to threaten to take her to jail and take the kids to DFCS.

"What's going on here, MA'AM?" I asked directing my attention to who I assumed was the caller, grabbing the little boy's hand. I remembered telling their mother she would be in a body bag if she continued to take the foolishness off the boyfriend she was defending. I prayed that day hadn't come to pass.

"It's their mother, officer." the older woman said. My heart sank and I feared the worst.

"I live next door, I'm the neighbor, Tracy. Wayne came running to the house banging on my door and told me his mom was in the tub and she was hurt, so I called you all to come as soon as I came from the house. Where is the ambulance? Maybe they can save her If they hurry!" she said looking around tapping her foot nervously.

"They are right behind me, Ma'am. While we are waiting for them, take me to her." I said.

"I can't. I can't lay eyes on her like that again!" she said starting to cry, looking at me sadly. "He destroyed that damn girl, he destroyed her!"

"Who destroyed her, ma'am? Did someone hurt her?" I asked.

"No, she did it to herself but he may as well have done it! Wayne can take you to her, I don't see why he hasn't shed a tear. He is a special little boy with some real strength. I can't stop crying and I'm three times his age." she said while wiping her tears, trying to gather her composure.

The house was beautiful on the outside, but the inside was filthy. It was pitch black, dark from no electricity; I had to be guided to the scene by the brave little boy I took for some ice cream. I knew he was special and wise beyond his years when he steered the conversation to something else, every time I asked him about what was going on at home. He maneuvered around the conversation so naturally, I just knew that he would know his way around a conversation when he was older. I prayed that watching his mother be mistreated wouldn't damage him as a man because he had so much potential.

When we made it to the oversized bathroom, I flashed my light around, taking in the awe-inspiring room. My flashlight landed on a jacuzzi tub big enough to fit an entire family into; It may as well have just been a swimming pool. The water was dark red as if the tub was filled with Red Wine. Laying there looking peaceful enough to be sleeping, was the beautiful young lady I told to get out of her terrible situation months before. She was taking slow steady gasps like a fish out of water. I heard the ambulance crew rushing up the stairs, but they were clearly struggling to make it through the dark house.

"In here!" I called out as I wondered how the hell, she was even still breathing with the amount of blood it looked like she'd lost.

"Who did this to your mother, son?" I asked the little boy, grabbing his hand to take him from the scene and back down the stairs. He looked back at his mother as the paramedics were taking her out of the tub, as if he didn't want to leave her alone; It broke my heart that he had to witness his mother in this situation.

"Ma,am, can you hear me?" the EMT asked in the background as Wayne and I walked away.

"She's in the best hands, little buddy. Those people went to school for a very long time to make people feel better." I told him with a reassurance I didn't feel.

"You promise?" he asked me innocently.

"Of course, now I need you to do your part like a big boy and help me out. Who did this to your mama? Was it a man?" I asked him with my finger on my radio transmission button, ready to reach out to dispatch. I secretly hoped he would say yes so I could put out an arrest warrant on the low-down, son of a bitch the young lady spoke so highly of.

"No, my baby sisters were sleeping when I saw my daddy creep out of the door. I stayed awake because I wanted to go into my momma's room and be next to her when she cried, like she usually does when daddy leaves. Only this time, instead of hearing her cry, I heard the water run. I have heard the bath at all times before, because my mama loves to take baths; she even makes us take them." Wayne told me while frowning, as if his mother making him take a bath was the worst thing she could ever do to him. A laughed slipped out unexpectedly, but I quickly regained my serious composure when I thought about the situation at hand.

"It wasn't crazy for her to take a bath; it was crazy that she stayed in there so long and I didn't hear the water let out." he said to me sadly. "It's real loud when the water lets out and I always hear it, so I went to the bathroom to make sure she didn't fall asleep. I didn't want her skin to be wrinkly and ashy like mine when I stay in the water too long, so I was just going to wake her up. Only when I went in there, I couldn't wake her and I knew something wasn't right. I got scared and ran next door to get Ms. Tracey." He told me concluding his story.

I looked at him sadly knowing that this scene would be one he would never forget. I prayed that the young lady would live through this situation and realize how her love for that man affected not only her, but the people that cared about her as well.

"OK, well you did a good thing and I'm proud of you." I told Wayne while rubbing the top of his head, like I did the little league players I coached. He began to smile causing my heart to break even further. "Here's what we're going to do buddy, do you know where your grandma, auntie, or uncle lives?" I asked him.

"Besides Ms. Tracey and Mr. Tom, we only ever visit Ms. Arlene. I don't have a grandma, auntie or uncle." he replied.

"Well, Im going to take you and your sisters to Ms. Arlene, ok. Come sit in the passenger seat of my car until it's time to go; don't worry about your mama, she's gonna go and get better just for tonight."

As he sat in my car holding his little sister on his lap, Wayne knew that his daddy was responsible for everything. He was happy when Mayday left so he could stop hurting his mama and, making her cry. He just hated how unhappy his mother was when Mayday wasn't there. She was unhappy when he was there, and unhappy when he wasn't there; Wayne just didn't understand. What his 5-year-old mind did understand, was love. At that tender age he couldn't describe exactly what he was feeling, but he knew that he felt very strongly for his mother. He would do absolutely anything for her; It didn't matter what happened to him. While he knew he felt that extreme emotion towards his mother, he knew he felt the exact opposite for his father.

Wayne watched the ambulance wheel his mother out of the house on the rolling bed, as I talked to a crying, Ms. Tracey. He wiped his silent tears from his face with the back of one of his hands and continued to rub his sister's back with the other. He vowed at that moment that the man responsible for their hurt, would pay with his life.

Chapter Fourteen
Netta

"You can get through this, you will get through this." Ms. Arlene told me as she held me in her arms and rocked me. The kids had been living with her for a year, while I was locked away in a mental institution trying to regain my life back from Mason. I joined them when I was released four months prior. For the most part I had regained my life back. I started back working for the hotel and I was saving to get an apartment for me and my children. However, I had my moments when I would have terrible nightmares and wake up shaking like a drug addict. This was one of those moments.

"Are you ok, Mommy?" Terri asked me with concern, waking up from her sleep and wiping her eyes. Me and my three children shared a spacious room at Ms. Arlene's home in Decatur GA. Her son was grown with a wife and kids, so she had her 2-bedroom house to herself. When DCFS threatened to take my children before they locked me away in an institution, I knew that I could call on her to help.

"Yes, your mother is fine, we are going to the den to have grown people talk. Crawl under your brother and baby sister and go on back to sleep." Ms. Arlene told my daughter as she helped me up and we walked into the other room.

"I'm going to pour us a glass of wine and I want you to have a seat at the table for me." she told me as she headed into her connecting kitchen.

Her home wasn't as big as Mason's; She did not have stairs.

Instead she had a 2-bedroom, ranch styled home, that was flat all the way through. She didn't have a large front yard but she had a very big back yard, for the kids to play in. She had even gone out and bought the kids a puppy; an all-black Labrador named Mister. She had a sitting room with a chocolate covered, leather, two piece that was only for decoration, a large dining room with a chandelier light fixture and a big cherry wood dining table and four chairs. Her kitchen was small with a big window that overlooked the front yard, and a den area where people mostly sat in with a tv, and radio. The den was connected to her fenced in backyard. I loved her home. She had been living there for 20 years. I also loved the fact that she wasn't renting it; instead it was bought and paid for.

"Baby let me tell you a story." she started while handing me a glass of wine, placing her glass in front of her on the table. "Spousal abuse run's in my family, so I know what you are going through. When I was 15, I held my older sister's head to her body, that it detached from because her husband shot her in the head with his hunting rifle when she told him that she was going to leave him after years of torture. When I was 19, my sister became addicted to drugs because the father of her five children, beat her at the same time every night like clockwork. He would turn off the power in the apartment from the outside breaker box and nail the doors and windows shut, to watch her and the kids run around trying to hide from him like he was a sick sadistic serial killer. Every bone on her body has been broken at least once and some bones more than once. She jumped out of a window he didn't bolt because he wanted to see if she would be desperate enough to jump. She barely escaped, and has mental and physical scars to this day from the abuse she endured. My husband beat me when he was drunk in front of our son. Me and my younger sister both knew we didn't want to end up like our oldest sister, so we left." She said pausing to take a sip.

"I know that man was everything to you, Netta. I know you feel like he was the reason you woke up every morning and the reason you went to sleep every night; I know he saved you from a terrible situation at home. The reason he did that was because he wanted a victim that would be desperate and at his mercy. Abusers feed off torturing their victims, like bottom feeders feed off fish shit. The thing is, no matter who left or how it happened, you survived. You hear me?" she asked me while holding my face in her hands and looking me eye to eye.

"You survived Jeanette because you were supposed to; that man could have killed you or YOU could have killed yourself that night. Instead, here you are living and breathing. It's because your kids need you! They have been through so much already. Do you know that the first 7 years of your child's life shapes who they will be? Can you imagine the amount of damage you have done to your children? Especially Wayne. Do you want him to grow up and do, to women what he has watched be done to you?" she asked me as the tears streamed down my face.

I knew what she was trying to do; Her and I had this talk multiple times, but this was the first time that she told me about her sister's. She tried to keep me uplifted and she tried to keep me strong. I tried to be strong. I was sure it had to be what a heroin addiction felt like. I knew he was bad for me, yet every part of my body ached for him; wanted him, needed him.

"No," I told her. "I don't want Wayne to grow up and hurt women." I said as I thought about how he was conceived. The product of a rape, my mother's attempt to shove a metal clothes hanger up my ass to scrape him out; the odds were stacked against him from the beginning.

My lips said no, and my mind said no, but my heart still wanted Mason regardless of who got hurt in the process. Out of everything I had been through I still wanted Mason.

Chapter Fifteen
Mason

"You like how I suck that dick, don't you?" Clara said to Me while taking my dick out of her mouth to roll her tongue around the tip. She slapped it on her tongue while gripping my balls; the combination caused my eyes to roll to the back of my head, involuntarily.

"Yeah baby, put that trouser snake in your mouth and swallow him. MMMHH, yeah just like that, baby!" I told the heavy-set nurse I had been dating for 7 months. Yeah, I lost almost everything when Lacey left me but I still had my half of the company.

I met nurse, Carla Brady, while I was doing physical therapy at Grady Hospital. Being dead broke with one leg, no home, no car, and no visitors will show you who your real friends were. While At my lowest, I allowed myself to be vulnerable, and Carla and I'd became friends.

I reminisced on how we met as she continued to suck my soul from my body.

She saw me sitting in the smoking section outside of the hospital smoking a cigarette, crying while looking down at what used to be my right leg. I was so caught up in my private pity party, I didn't notice her until she started talking.

"You don't have to cry handsome; everything will be ok." she told me as she sat next to me.

"Yeah I know, I know." I said quickly startled by her presence. Trying to gain my composure, I wiped the tears from my face.

I knew a man wasn't supposed to cry; society never hesitated to remind me of the strength I was supposed to have. What society failed to realize was the fact that, even though I was born with testosterone and a dick, I still had feelings and emotions. I knew that I was mentally slipping away because the old me was too sharp to let someone get that close to me without noticing their presence, but I was becoming too tired to care. I really did wish the Italians would have taken my life because I didn't have anything left to live for.

"I know the world says men, particularly Black men, aren't allowed to cry but I call bullshit, brother. You have feelings and emotions just like any other human being and you can be upset at this curveball life has thrown at you." she said taking the words out of my head, as if I had spoken them aloud.

She was a heavy-set woman; dark skin and chunky with a pretty face. She had more hair than I had ever seen on the head of a black woman, dimples, and a wide gorgeous smile. She smelled good and her all white nurse's uniform made her look like an angel. She wore her size 14 with confidence and seemed to embrace the fact that she had more curves than other women. She joked that it would take a man with big hands to handle all she had to offer, and that was because of her size and how well she handled her business.

"I'm Clara, I have been watching you for a while and I dig how you carry yourself." she told me while reaching out her hand for me to shake it. I looked at her and paused before I responded.

The old me would have been offended that a chick that wasn't all that and a bag of chips had the nerve to step to me. The new me saw her as an opportunity. I had no home, no car, one leg, piece of a sinking company, and hospital bills racking up; I would need all the help I could get.

"Yeah, I been seeing you see me. I think you're pretty but I'm

My Mother's Man

just in a bad place right now; trying to get used to this new me. I hate to look down and see nothing there where my leg used to be." I told her sadly, while holding my head down. If she wanted to see a broken vulnerable man, I could play the role. The fact that I had an ulterior motive gave me the upper hand. It was the control I craved, and I would control this situation like I had all the others.

I began to break down and let my emotional floodgates open, as I opened up to her. I cried as I told her how hurt I was; how my wife left me as soon as she found out that my leg was gone and served me with divorce papers and the ring I'd bought for her with my entire life savings. I told her about Netta, the mother of my two children, who waited until I went to work on an out of town construction project and took everything from me, including my two precious daughters. I told her about my wife before Lacey, who took advantage of the fact that I was a poor black boy from the projects, and she treated me like I was her slave instead of her husband.

When I was through with my story Nurse Carla was in tears as she rubbed my back softly. "I can't say I understand you because I have never been in that situation, but I understand lost and I'm here for you if you need anything." she said as she lit her cigarette. As if she recovered a long-lost forgotten thought, she snapped her two fingers together and asked me, "did they tell you about the new prosthetics program the hospital has been working on?"

"No, that's fake stuff, right? I haven't heard anything about it. What is the program about?" I asked her while wiping the tears from my face, wishing there were cameras in the bushes. The performance I had just put down was big screen worthy; I deserved to be on the big screen.

"Wellllll, the hospital is doing a program where they are offering discounts on prosthetic limbs to the first 20 patients who sign up and pay the 3,000 dollar deposit." she said as if she'd said the deposit was 50 bucks.

"The total cost of the limb starts at 7,000 dollars, but if you can

put the 3,000 dollars down the hospital will pay the remaining balance!" She said jumping for joy when truthfully, she had only made me feel worse.

I didn't have a dime to my name at that moment; I didn't even know where I would live when I was released from the hospital. Mensloe had a small efficiency apartment that I could probably sleep on the floor of; everything I had left, I put into the loft with Layla when I moved in with her. I understood now more than ever that you couldn't judge a book by its cover because I was sitting there like a bum, when I lived in the lap of luxury, drove fine cars, wore expensive threads, and saved up for a nice house, that I let go down the drain while I travelled and enjoyed the good life with Layla.

I didn't know what my future held. I had no idea that I would lose her and all the perks that came from being with her. Worst case scenario, I felt that I'd always have my half of the business, and I could always get money from that. However, my construction company was contractual; which meant no contracts no money. I was literally at ground zero.

"Well Mama, I dig you looking out for a brother and I will keep that in mind if I ever come up on a miracle. Losing my leg has cost me everything, so I don't exactly have 3,000 dollars laying around." I told her with a sad, half smile and a quivering lip.

"Well, let me see what my savings look like, maybe I can help you." she said while wiping her tears and looking at me; I smiled at her. When I was released from the hospital, I moved into her huge apartment, I had been there since.

My cum leaving my body, hitting the back of her throat startled me from my walk down memory lane. I gripped the back of her head and slammed my pelvis into her face, as every muscle in my body spasmed and convulsed. I didn't know if I was having a seizure or going into shock, as she ate my dick like one of those high calorie meals she loved. I hated to fuck her, so a lot of times I would tell her to bend over so I could drill her from the back. She assumed that hitting it from the back was my favorite position when truthfully, I just didn't want to see her face; it was easier to imagine that she was someone else. I had to give credit where it was due though, her head game was vicious and it was the only thing she was good for, besides going to work all day, every day to provide my every need and desire.

Chapter Sixteen
<u>Netta</u>

♪ *Sun in the sky you know how I feel*
Breeze driftin' on by you know how I feel
(refrain:)
It's a new dawn
It's a new day
It's a new life
For me
And I'm feeling good ♪

For the first time in my life I felt independent and strong. After the long talk I had with Ms. Arlene at her dinner table, I knew it was time to be a better mother and better example. I didn't want to continue to pass the dysfunction I grew up in, down to my children. So, I gave into the help I had been resisting.

Ms. Arlene taught me how to drive and helped me save up for my first car. It was a small used Toyota Camry and it wasn't the prettiest thing but, it was enough for me and the kids to get around. After the car, I was approved for federal housing for low income mothers. I met all the qualifications and with Ms. Arlene's help, I completed the application and gathered the necessary documents. I was able to get an apartment and food stamps so that I could feed myself and the kids. After a lot of practice and willpower I learned how to read and write small words; I was more, proud of that accomplishment than anything. I felt like less of a mother when my kids wanted me to help them with their homework or read the great report the teacher sent home, and I couldn't understand any of it. Faking the funk only lasted for so long.

I stopped in the grocery store to grab some chicken, rice, juice, and snacks for the kids, when I laid eyes on him. He was standing next to a big woman that had to be 3 times my size, with a nurse's uniform on. He didn't look like himself, instead of his usual sexy threads he had on a stretched out t-shirt and a pair of jeans. His most noticeable accessory was a cane stick. I wondered why the hell he was leaning on a cane stick like an old man; maybe he'd hurt his ankle.

As if he could hear my thoughts he looked up and caught my gaze. The world fell from around me and I felt like we were the only two people in the store. My heart began to beat faster and my palms began to sweat. My nipples hardened like someone had suddenly turned on the air conditioner, and my pussy begin to throb. He was the last man that touched me, stroked me, penetrated me. He was the only man I'd voluntarily let inside of me; he was my everything. He smiled the smile I loved so much, and chills ran down my spine. Lord why was I created to be so weak for this man?

I turned away from him and ran up the aisle in the opposite direction. I heard a clacking noise behind me, and I knew he was following me; struggling to catch up. I pretended to be in the cereal aisle looking at different brands, even though I knew he was walking towards me; I could feel him.

"Hey Net, how you doing?" he asked me sweetly and smiled.

It was as if the monster that had beaten me, verbally abused me, left me with his children, left me in his home to get evicted, gave me numerous STD'S, and got me approached and jumped by his side hoes, never existed. This was the man I had fallen in love with. This was the MayDay that rescued me from a fucked-up situation, defended my son against abuse, and gave us a place to stay when my mother showed me her door. I felt forever indebted to him.

"I'm doing good, working and finally driving." I said proudly. "Got a place for me and the kids, about to go pick up Bonnie and Terri; Wayne goes to the big kids' school now, so he catches the school bus and it brings him in front of the house."

"Oh ok. How are you managing a household and bills and you can't read?" he asked me with a slight laugh.

"I been learning how, but I'm going to get on; I hope everything has been fine with you. Keep your head up and be safe." I said knowing he was being shady. As I turned to walk away, he grabbed me by my hand.

"I didn't mean it in a bad way, I'm proud of you Net. I'm glad that it took me to make you into the woman you are now because without me, that wouldn't have happened. You do know that, right?" he asked.

"Yes, I know Mason, I owe it all to you. So, if ever you need me for anything, I don't mind helping you."

As if those were the magic words, he grabbed the basket out of my hand and headed to the front. I followed behind him closely, unsure of what he was about to do.

"Aye," he said to the heavy-set woman he was standing with before he walked over to me. "This is Netta, who I was telling you about. She is the mother of my children, and you been good to me, but I need to make my family work. Keep your head up." he told her as he walked to the other cashier's line.

"WAIT! You told me she abandoned your ass and left you high and dry! So just like that, you just walk in the store with me and walk out with her?? I bought you that leg with all my savings, at least give me that back. I didn't take you for this type of man, Mason!" she said sounding hurt, walking up on him. She grabbed him by his shirt and before things could get further, the police officer in the grocery store walked over to them.

"Look Ms., what's this? What is the problem here?" he asked.
"That is assault to grab someone or touch them without their permission. I don't want to have to arrest you" he told her in warning.

"I understand that, officer. I am a nurse over at Grady Memorial Hospital, I'm not a hoodlum ghetto girl but this man has on a 3,000-dollar prosthetic leg, that I paid for with every dime of my savings. If he no longer wants to be with me that's fine. However, he is going to give me back the leg I bought before he limps off into the sunset with another woman!" she said angrily. Her tone had begun to rise, causing the people in the store to stop what they were doing to listen in on the drama.

"Ms., If you gave him the property as a gift, he is under no legal obligation to return it. If you want It back, you will have to take him to small claims court and sue him for the property." the officer said calmly.

"IT'S FINE, YOUR ASS GOING TO REAP WHAT YOU SOW, MASON VACTOR! TRUST ME YOU GOING TO GET YOURS, LOW LIFE MOTHERFUCKER!" she said getting out of character; completely ignoring the officer while jumping back into Mason's face. The policeman quickly grabbed her and, led her in the opposite direction before the scene got uglier.

"I DON'T CARE WHAT YOU GOT TO SAY ABOUT ME, LADY! I LOVE THIS GIRL RIGHT HERE, SHE'S MY WORLD AND THE MOTHER OF MY KIDS! I WOULD NEVER PICK YOU OVER HER!" he said more for the nosey crowd, and my benefit, than as a response to the woman because she was already out of the door.

I smiled when I heard some women commenting on what happened.

"He must really love her and his kids!" one of the women said.

"Yeah, that's what I'm talking about! I wish my baby daddy, Kip, would stand up for me like that in front of these homewrecking women."

"There really are some good brother's out here." the cashier said to the women as she rang up their groceries.

"If he such a good man why did he wait until after the girl left to say how much he loves the other one?" said an older woman under her breath, while waiting in line to pay for her Sunday dinner, knowing a snake when she saw one.

∞∞∞

"It's smaller than MY taste," Mason said while touching his chest. "But, its ok for you and the kids. I know y'all miss that big ole house I had y'all in overlooking the lake and shit, but this will do." he finished as I gave him the tour of my apartment. He'd spoke nothing but negativity since he'd gotten into my passenger seat.

This old car has a lot of mileage, he pointed out first.

It's small, how do you and all the kids fit in here?

Why are you driving with your foot on the brake like you're afraid of the road?

Who taught you to drive scary? He asked more concerned about being in my business, than acknowledging how excited his daughter was to see him when she saw him in the passenger seat. I made her contain her excitement until we made it home, but the minute we got into the house she was all over him.

"DADDYYYYYYY!!!!" she yelled excitedly and jumped into his lap.

I smiled as I saw him smiling and kissing her on her forehead. I never had a father's love but it looked precious, and I was glad my daughter had the opportunity to experience it. Bonnie did her usual and played with her toys in indifference; Mason hadn't been in her life consistently enough for her to know who he was exactly.

After I gave him the tour, he rested comfortably on my couch; the one I scoured through countless thrift stores to find, and he made statements about how uncomfortable and lumpy it was. His feet were propped up on the matching ottoman and his daughter was in his lap when Wayne made it home.

"How was your day?" I asked him like I did every day when he ran through the door.

I may have not been the smartest person but I was an open book with my kids. I wanted them to feel like they could come home and tell me about whatever took place at school that day. My question fell on deaf ears for Wayne. The only movement he'd made since walking into the door, was his usual motion of kicking it closed behind him. Instead of answering my question he stood, cemented to the hard wood floor. If looks could kill Mason would have been sprawled out on the floor. He stared at the man as if he were a pile of dog shit.

Sensing his glare, Mason tore his attention from the tv and turned to look at Wayne. He never broke eye contact as he stared right back at the 7-year-old. He placed soft kisses on his daughter's forehead with a light smirk on his face. I looked back and forth between them and wondered if I had made a big mistake by allowing Mason to come back into our lives.

Chapter Seventeen
Netta

"YEAH THROW THAT PUSSY BACK ON THIS DICK. YOU DONE GOT OUT OF PRACTICE BUT IMA STRETCH IT BACK OUT!"

Mayday said to me as he slammed into me hard from the back. He was banging my back out of place and I swear it felt like he was trying to dislocate something. I didn't know if he was trying to make up for the fact that he only had one leg, so he felt the need to be extra rough, but he was doing more than necessary ramming into my stomach. I bit down on my bottom lip to try not to complain; Mason hated when I complained.

"MMHM, YEAH BABY IT'S STILL GOOD!" I moaned to him lying through my teeth.

I usually enjoyed sex with him, but it had been a while for me because of his disappearing act, so I would have appreciated it if he could go a little easier. I knew not to tell him that though; anytime I made any suggestions he would slap me and do the exact opposite of whatever I suggested. I tried to slightly scoot up to position myself to take it better but he grabbed me by my waist to hold me in place, as he continued to bang like a damn hammer hitting a nail.

"SHITTTTTT, IM COMMINGGG NETTA!" he said dramatically; so loud that I knew my kids heard it and half the damn neighborhood too.

My kids' rooms were closer in this apartment than his

house; and I didn't want my son to hear me getting to it. It didn't matter at that point, I just wanted him to cum so he could end the torture.

"ME TOO, DADDY! ME TO!" I said to him like he'd taught me to. He told me that it turned him on to hear me say that, even if It wasn't true. "DADDY DON'T CUM IN ME, I WANT YOU TO PUT IT IN ON MY BACK!" I said in the sexiest voice I could.

Truthfully, I just didn't want any more damn kids with him. He didn't help me with the two daughters he had ALREADY given me; there was no way in hell I was trying to be pregnant, fucking up the routine I had established. It was hard being 23 with three kids and my oldest only being 7. Aside from Ms. Arlene I didn't have anyone to depend on because my family turned their backs on me the day I'd left my mother's house. Now that everything was going smoothly, I didn't have time to be sick, keeping appointments, missing work, and everything else that came with a newborn. The kids were depending on me and I had let them down so much already.

"NAW, IMA CUM IN YOU LIKE I SAID, I WANT A SON!"

As soon as he said those words, I felt his body tense up. He held me in place and assaulted my pelvis to let me know he was doing exactly what he said he would. After he huffed and puffed, he fell next to me on the bed satisfied. I was glad that at least one of us was satisfied. As quick as the thought entered my mind it left, as I leaned on one shoulder and rubbed his face. I admired his full lips, deep dimples, and chocolate skin.

"Baby you have a son. Wayne is your son, you're the only father he knows." I said to him sweetly.

"I'm not his daddy! You were raped to make him and his ass probably going to grow up to be a rapist himself, he ain't got my blood!" he replied disrespectfully.

I looked up at the ceiling; I hated when he talked crazy about my only son.

"Whatever; let's talk about what the hell happened to your leg, Mason." I said choosing my battles wisely, getting straight to the question that had been bothering me, since he'd had the argument with the woman at the store. He sighed.

"Well, honestly I was just in the wrong place at the wrong time." he said as his eyes filled with tears. I had never seen Mason cry in all the years we had been together.

"It's ok, get it out." I told him while running my fingers through his chest hair the way he liked it.

"I'm just a black man trying to make it, Netta. I just happen to be at a store and got kidnapped by a group of white men. I knew they were white because even though they had on masks, I could see their wrists when their gloves moved. They took me to an abandoned place and beat me for hours, claiming that I didn't pay back a debt. I told them over and over, that I had no idea what they were talking about and that I'd never been to Vegas or knew no high-powered man. I'm a Georgia boy born and raised; you know that Net." he said to me sadly.

I nodded my head fast in response.

"I told them that I had a woman I loved and 2 beautiful daughters that needed their daddy; I began to beg for my life. I'm a proud man but my kids didn't ask to be here, so if I had to beg someone to keep me here for them, then dammit I didn't mind! They asked me would I rather limp back to my family or let them bury me in a pine box. I told them to do what they had to do because I wouldn't leave my family." he said with tears streaming down his face, freely.

I had begun to cry as well. I knew that his story was true because he told it with too much emotion. I also knew how vain Mason was, and I could honestly say that he would have rather been dead than walk around less than perfect. He must have really missed me and the kids for him to go through all, of that pain just to get back to us.

"After they cut off my leg, they took me to the hospital so I wouldn't bleed to death. I guess they decided to have some type of mercy on a poor, negro man. The part that hurt more than anything was the fact that they left a note by my hospital bed admitting that they had the wrong man. They told me the man they **thought** I was, had pissed off a very powerful, wealthy man, so they were coming to collect his due. They told me they later discovered that I wasn't that man, I just looked a hell of a lot like him because, **all of us nigger boys look so much alike.** They also said they had some powerful connections so if I told anyone, the woman I love as well as my kids were going to die. You saw how those people did our ancestors, they evil and they mean what they say. So, I didn't call no police or make no reports or nothing! They left a few hundred dollars in the note and told me to buy myself a fake leg because those things are expensive. I guess that was their way of apologizing, but they can't give me back my leg so damn their apology!" Mason said emotionally.

I held him as he cried like a baby. I was so afraid for my son, who was a black boy that would grow up to be a black man. I couldn't understand why a group of people hated another group of people so bad, just because of the color of their skin. We had come so far as a people and been through so much, all we wanted to do was live and be happy like everyone else.

"I stayed away from you and the kids to make sure they really were done messing with me. When I felt safe again, I tried to come and find you but I didn't have no luck. That was God that brought you back to me, Net. Like you said, we matched blood. You are mine and I am yours forever. Even after we both dead and gone, we will always belong to each other."

"You're right, Mayday. I don't know why you left but I understand why you stayed gone. You hurt me and the kids so bad; we love you." I told him. "We nee-" Before I could finish telling him that we needed him I heard my daughter, Terri, screaming, "MAMMMMMAAAAAA!" Causing me to jump out of the bed and run to her faster than I knew I could.

"WHATS WRONG, BABY? IS EVERYTHING OK??" I yelled.

When I made it to the bedroom that my two daughters shared, what I saw caused my heart to sink beneath my feet. Standing over my 2-year-old daughter's bed, with a gun pointed at her head, was the heavy-set woman that I saw earlier that day with Mason in the grocery store.

I immediately dropped to my knees

Chapter Eighteen
Netta

♪ *So I'm telling you these things*
To let you know how much I love that man
And woman to woman
I think you'll understand
How much I'll do to keep him

Woman to woman
If you've ever been in love
Then you know how I feel
And woman to woman
Now, if you were in my shoes
Wouldn't you have done the same thing too

Oh, oh, woman to woman
Can't you see where I'm coming from
Woman to woman
Ain't that the same thing you would've done ♪

My two-year-old daughter played with the woman's gun as if it were a toy and not the end of her life staring back at her. She smiled at my daughter and rubbed one of her two afro puffs; I often joked that her puffs were the biggest thing on her little body.

"Look, I don't know what you have going on with Mason, but my baby doesn't have nothing to do with this, ma'am; she just a baby." I told her looking her eye to eye.

She looked crazy as hell as she smiled at me and sat down next to my baby on her twin bed; I wasn't sure why the hell Mason would even deal with somebody that looked like her. Her hair was all over her head, she still had on her white nurse's uniform, and her thick white shoes.

"Please, just let my baby go." I begged her. "You can hash this shit out with Mason; he is the person you're mad at it" I tried reasoning.

"I Just don't understand why I deserve this shit!" she said back to me in defeat.

"I see why he loves you and had kids with you; I mean look at you! That gorgeous skin, gorgeous face, and perfect body; I WASN'T BLESSED WITH NONE OF THAT SHIT!" she said screaming at me.

"Just calm down, sister. We can talk about this; we can talk through this." I told her while raising my hands in surrender. When she started screaming, she began to jab Bonnie in the head with the gun, causing my little bun bun to cry.

"I'll calm down but I ain't your sister, bitch! I don't want to hear that sister and brother black power shit! I see people in the emergency room every day at my job and the people that usually put them there, is their own damn kind. Our own damn kind! What this here about, is the fact that the man in your bed belongs to me; I been taking care of his ass for almost a year and he thinks it's ok to walk into a store with me and out of that same store with you?! I have 5 cents to my name, *sister.* 5 FUCKIN, CENT! I emptied out my savings account on him. I bought him that leg for 3,000 dollars, I bought him clothes, shoes, and draws for his ass. When he woke up in the middle of the night crying about that funky ass leg, talking about he needed a vacation to clear his mind, I TOOK HIS ASS TO A RESORT IN FLORIDA FOR 3 WEEKS!" she said slamming the gun against her own head in despair, as tears ran down her face.

"Are you ok mama?" my son asked from the doorway of the

bedroom. Clara's head quickly popped up to see who had spoken and I turned the top half of my body in his direction quickly; almost snapping my back in half.

"Mama is fine, ok. This is mama's friend and we are talking about grown folks stuff, so go back to bed for me." I told him while stressing the urgency of him leaving with my facial expression.

With the constant abuse and neglect, Wayne had already seen more than a 7-year-old should have. I didn't want to scar him any more than he already was. I could imagine what damage this would do to Terri; she was sitting in her bed clutching her favorite bear close to her chest. I knew she'd peed on herself because she always peed when she was afraid. She knew this lady wasn't a friend and something wasn't right.

"Ok mommy, but like you say to me, tell your lil friend it's too late to play because you have school in the morning." he said wiping his eyes with the back of his hands and walking away.

I choked back a sob. Clara waited until he walked away. Rolling her eyes upward she finished.

"Like I was saying, his lazy ass been on my sofa, I have been providing for him! His construction company ain't had not ONE contract; **ZERO**! I spent all my savings and I've been working doubles at the hospital, overtime, my coworker's shifts and all, to make ends meet and replenish my savings. You know what he told me about you? That you took his children, cleared his house out, and disappeared while he was on a construction work assignment out of state. Why would he want to go back to a bitch like that, huh? Every woman he has ever loved has turned their backs on him. Both of his wives left when he needed them most and so did you!" She said confusing the hell out of me.

"So, do you think it's fair for me to just let you and these crumb snatchers take my man? WE WAS WORKING ON A FAMILY!" she screamed while putting the gun back to the head of my

2-year-old.

"What the hell all this screaming about?" Mayday asked as he entered the bedroom, until he laid eyes on Clara. "SHIT!" he screamed and jumped back into the hallway while putting his hands in the air.

Clara turned the gun in his direction.

"So, you really thought it was just over with, Mason? Just like that?"

"Clare bear,"

"DON'T FUCKIN CLARE BEAR, ME!" she screamed "IM ABOUT TO KILL EVERY LAST ONE OF YOUR KIDS, IMA KILL THIS BITCH, THEN ME AND YOU ARE GOING TO RIDE TO MEXICO AND START OUR LIFE OVER!" she yelled at him.

"Well only the two girls are mine baby, the lil boy she already had before I met her. So, you can kill his ass and kill her. Then me, you, and my girls can just go to Mexico and you can be their new mama. I told you I'm going to marry you, you will be a good mama. This bitch here," he said pointing at me. "she can't even read! I only pretended to want her so I could come and see my kids. I would never leave you for her after she left me the way she did." he said looking at me with disgust.

My heart skipped. Less than 30 minutes ago he was knee deep inside of me, now I was the worthless bitch that couldn't read and kept him from his kids??

"I can't fuckin believe you! We've been together since I was 15 years old. You would really let a woman kill me and my son in cold blood just to save your ass?" I asked him in confusion.

"Well baby as you can see, my ass is already saved. What you need to determine is if you want your daughters to continue to live. Me and my girl are going to Mexico. I know I'm asking a lot of her to raise another woman's kids, but my baby loves me, so I know she doesn't mind being a mother to my daughters." he said looking at her affectionately.

I looked back to see her reaction, she was smiling from ear to ear.

"Yeah baby, I'm going to have to teach them to be better women than their mother. She's beautiful, but beauty don't get you every damn thing. What kind of bitch this old can't even read?! Thank God we are catching them young. I have plenty of time to teach them how to be real women. The same way my parents taught me." she said wiping her tears and running mascara from her chubby cheeks.

"I'm going to get her lil nappy head ass son in here, so they can die together." Mason said.

"Mason, please don't do this! If you don't want to be with me and you want her, that's fine. You and her, can go right now; I have been raising my kids alone while you were gone. I won't hunt you down to help me, I never have. Just please let me and my son live." I told him.

The situation itself was answering the question I asked myself earlier that day. He hadn't been back in our lives 24 hours and he was already bringing us heartache and drama, all over again. The tears wouldn't stop coming.

"I mean, my baby is the lady in charge and if she wants you done then you done." he said unapologetically. "Baby, do you want us to just take my kids and let this bitch and her lil son, live?" he asked her like it didn't matter what her decision was.

"Well, honestly," she started

"FREEZE!" I heard a police officer scream from the doorway.

Clara turned the gun from me, to the officer. I began to sob harder at how smart my son was. When he walked away wiping his eyes in the opposite direction of his room, I knew exactly what he was going to do. I just didn't know that Mason would advocate for the death of me and my child the way he had.

"YEAH, THAT'S HER OFFICER!" he said to the police officer,

pointing at a now open-mouthed Clara.

"This woman is obsessed with me, officer. She tried to get with me the other day and I told her I had a woman and some beautiful kids at home. She got mad and followed me home; SHE'S SICK!!!" he told the police officer with the same sincerity he had when he told me the story of being in the wrong place, at the wrong time, looking like the wrong man.

"YOU SON OF A BITCH!" Clara screamed out, firing the gun in Mason's direction.

Chapter Nineteen
__Netta__

♪ I feel nice, like sugar and spice
I feel nice, like sugar and spice
So nice, so nice, I got you

When I hold you in my arms
I know that I can't do no wrong
And when I hold you in my arms
My love won't do you no harm ♪

"Bring your ass on, Net. We only leaving for 3 days, not 3 years!" Mason yelled over the blaring music from inside of the car as I kissed my babies, goodbye.

"I love you, mama!" Wayne said to me, while squeezing me like he would never see me again.

"Be a good boy and help Ms. Arlene with your sisters, ok? We only going to the beach for 3 days, I will be back before you miss me." I said to him smiling.

"Hmmph!" Ms. Arlene said as she stood in the doorway and shot daggers through her eyes, at Mason.

I knew she didn't mind looking after the kids for me, it was me leaving and going with Mason that made her angry. She tried for days to talk me out of it but I explained to her like he explained it to me. We needed some romantic, adult time away from the kids for a few days, to make our relationship stronger. I had been working like a slave, so I needed to rest and relax.

"Have fun and be careful, please!" Ms. Arlene said to me, holding my hand a second longer than necessary.

The girls were busy playing and running around with the dog, Mister. I didn't think my absence would hit them until later. I also felt that both Wayne and Ms. Arlene were being a little dramatic.

"I will be careful and I love you both very much. I'm going to kick my feet up for a few days and get some me time in, but I will be back soon." I told them, waving my hand and walking away.

I had been taking care of Mason hand and foot while still trying to keep the household schedule afloat. Dealing with Mason was like having a fourth child, he was always needing and requesting something; not to mention the fact that I had to constantly change out the bandages for the wound in his side; the site where the bullet had gone straight through the day he was shot by the crazy nurse. The responding officer fired the fatal shot that ended her life, but deep down I felt sorry for her. I had been used and abused by Mason enough to know that his love was the worst thing for you; It could hook you worse than any drug.

The gunshot wound needed constant cleaning and fresh bandages, so infection wouldn't spread through his body. I think the worst part of cleaning it was the terrible odor that smelled up the entire house when I removed the bandages. I didn't want the kids to inhale it not knowing what the effects were, so I always told them to go outside and play when I cleaned his wound. To say I needed a break was an understatement. So, when Mason suggested that me and him go to the beach for a few days to recharge and reconnect, I thought it was a great idea; it would be our first vacation together.

"We outta here, my beauty queen." Mason said to me, giving me his crooked smile and mashing the gas; heading towards the interstate.

My heart fluttered. I decided that I wouldn't bring up the hurtful things he had said until we made it to our destination. I had forgiven him, but I wanted to talk to him again about what took place that night in our daughter's bedroom. My spirit wasn't convinced fully that he'd just said those things to keep Carla at bay, until we came up with a plan; like he said.

Ms. Arlene

"So, how is she?" Officer Peddle Way asked me while sitting across from me at my kitchen table. He had been checking on Netta and the kids since he dropped them off the night, she tried to end her life.

Whenever she needed something and I didn't have it, I would call him and he would come through with it. He always told me to keep the fact that he was there for her between me and him, but I wanted to shout it from the mountain tops. I always told him that knowing someone else cared for her may have been the strength she needed to leave Mason's no-good ass alone for good. Sometimes women did desperate things out of loneliness. He would always tell me that she needed more time to get Mason out of her system, so he wanted to continue to observe until the time was right. I think it was also the officer in him that wanted to be sure she was done with Mason's troublesome ass, before he inserted himself into the situation. He had too much to lose, he couldn't allow Netta to get him into any mess because of a past she wasn't ready to let go of.

"She's ok, got fresh damn scars around her face, so he's still kicking her ass; she just ain't telling me about it no more. She knows how disappointed I was when she told me she'd not only accepted his trifling behind back, but she let him move in with her after all the mess he took her through. Then as if it doesn't get no worse, he almost gets her, and the babies killed because he can't control the women, he's dealing with! You want some pie baby?" I yelled out to him from the kitchen as I poured him a glass of juice.

My Mother's Man

"Yeah, I will take some. I'm glad that she's ok, Ms. Arlene. That could have gone worst." PeddleWay said to me.

"More and more I want to throw caution to the wind and just approach her to tell her how I feel. Maybe when the joker was gone that was my opportunity to pursue her. It's just I wanted to give her some space while she was rebuilding herself. You kept me afloat on all the things she was accomplishing and I was afraid that she would turn me down because she was still discovering herself. If I would have known that he was going to find a way right back to her I wouldn't have waited so long. I fear that each day she's with that fool he's damaging her more and more. I can be the man she needs but I could tell the day I met her, when she defended a man that got her jumped on and hurt, that he had his hooks in her so deep, it's going to take a miracle for her to give another man a chance."

"I can't say you're wrong, Ron." I told him. "Even now, it's been years since I've been with my son's father, but all that I went through with him has me terrified to give another man a real chance with me. I pray that the same thing doesn't happen to her. She's so young and beautiful. She can offer the right man so much. She can offer you so much. You and Netta are alike in so many ways, both caring and sweet. I don't get much company since my son moved away to California with his wife and my grandbaby, so Netta is the daughter that I never had and those kids; Lord those kids are my grandbabies, I would do anything to see them safe." I told him setting the pie and juice in front of him, at the table, when he got a call over the radio

"RADIO TO OFFICER 56!" The radio crackled loudly from his shoulder.

"GO AHEAD RADIO." he replied. "That's my cue I will stop back by to grab the pie before I head home." he said standing and giving me a kiss on the cheek; he was such a dream and he would be perfect for Net.

When he ran out the door, I remembered that I wanted

to tell him that she had gone on a road trip to Savannah with Mason. I wanted him to keep his ears open for anything he may have heard coming across that radio. I didn't trust Mason's snake ass as far as I could throw him.

Chapter Twenty
Netta

"You wanna be shot, cut, or beat?" Mason asked me as we stood in the woods in the middle of nowhere. I was as naked as the day as I was born and I had no idea where we were, because I couldn't read the names of the towns on the green expressway signs.

"May- Mason please, I just want to make it back home to my babies, our babies; they need me they need their momma!" I said to him crying and attempting to cover myself.

He told me we were going to the beach and that it was only 4 hours away. We had been riding for longer than 4 hours; I knew something wasn't right when we made it to a dark stretch of highway, and he pulled to the side of the road.

"I gotta piss like a racehorse. Come and run in these woods with me to watch my back." he told me smiling at me. The highway was so dark I couldn't see further than the lights shined, so I would have rather he pissed on himself than getting out of the car at that moment.

"Baby, just ride down a little further." I suggested.

"That ain't what I told you. Net! This what the hell I be talking about!" he said angrily turning the car off and opening the door to step out. I undid my seat belt, reached for the flashlight and got out of the car. I would take my chances with him out in the woods versus being left here in the dark, inside of a car, alone.

"I'm coming, I'm coming." I told him as I followed him into the trees.

"Hold the light steady!" he told me as I shined the light on his big, black dick, while he shook the piss off.

"Actually, come get on your knees and suck this big boy." he told me with a sexy side smile.

"Baby, you always playing. Both of our ass going to get ate up out here by these bugs and who knows what else is out here in the dark. As soon as we make it back to the car, I'm all yours." I told him laughing and turning to walk back in the direction of the car.

I felt him before I heard the twig underneath his foot snap. He hit me in the back of my head so hard, the only thing I could do was fall face first on the ground. I lost control of the flashlight and it went flying in the opposite direction. He kicked me in the back with his one strong leg and picked up the flashlight.

"Stand your ass up!" he said aggressively while pointing the flashlight at me like a police officer. I used my hands to raise my body onto wobbly knees and then shaky legs. I was terrified of what he may do to me out there while we were all alone. In the blink of an eye, being alone with him went from pure peace to a terrifying hell, that I prayed I would make it out of.

"You hardheaded and you don't listen! The real reason I brought you out here was because I think you done forgot who the hell, I am! Yeah, I lost a limb and a few material thangs, but I'm still that nigga who your soul belongs to!"

"I haven't forgotten, May!"

"I wasn't finished, Shut up! This what the hell I be talking about!" he said.

"Now, you done forgot, so ima help you remember!" he said smiling. "You got three options, just three." he said putting up his three fingers like a toddler learning to count.

"One, I could beat you, Two I could stick you," he said lifting up his pants leg to show the knife he kept strapped to his leg. "or, I could shoot you." he said shrugging his shoulders and lifting his shirt, to show a gun tucked in his waist band.

This had to be a recent purchase, because since he had been living with me, I had never laid eyes on a gun. Maybe it was a purchase with this specific scene in mind. The thought that he planned out this entire scenario, hurt me more than any of the times he'd ever hit me. How could I love someone so much, who obviously had so much hate for me in his heart?

"Mason, I choose none of that stuff. What do I have to do to show you that I love you more than anyone in my life? I will stop giving you back talk and remember my place. You wanted to teach me a lesson, well I done learned; I promise I have." I prayed silently that I could get through to him and he would have a heart for me.

"I could do all 3 to your ass and leave you out here for the deer's, rats, and bears to have at you. Answer my damn question which one you want?" he said with aggravation.

Looking around at the surrounding darkness knowing I had no way out of the situation, I went with the choice that I usually went with, without him asking.

"BEAT ME, JUST BEAT ME!" I screamed at him with all my pent-up anger and aggression. I prayed that my anger would shield me from the blows to lessen the pain, as I dropped to my knees and attempted to shield my face. My prayers went unanswered like they usually did.

"You done got you a lil job, a lil car, and a lil cheap apartment, now your ass forgetting that I run this!" he said while hitting me in the face with the flashlight, tree branches, his wooden leg, a brick, or anything else he could get his hand on quickly.

I made the mistake of reflexively hitting him back. My reflexes should have known that any movement during his beatings would anger him more. If at first I thought it couldn't get any worse, it began to. After each hit, I felt him tug at a piece of my clothing. When he was done, I lay completely naked and shaking in a ball on a bed of dead leaves. Every piece of my body including the strands of hair on my head hurt. I wished I would die; I wished it was the end of my pathetic life. I knew Ms. Arlene would try to protect my kids with her life, but since Mason was Terri and Bonnie's blood daddy, he would get custody of my girls. Wayne would grow up without me and his sisters, because there was no way Mason would let him get a bond with the sisters he adored. Mason despised him too much.

As if he wasn't done humiliating me, he proceeded to live out some sick fantasy of fucking me every way but the right way, in those woods. I didn't know where I was, how to get home; hell, how to even make it back to the car. I was completely at his mercy. After he was finished, he gathered himself and my clothes from the ground.

"Follow me!" he said to me nonchalantly, as if I had willingly given myself to him out there in the cold dark woods.

He waited for me to stand up and walk to his side; he then grabbed my hand and began to walk back to the car. Clearly this had not been his first time there. How the hell would a man born and raised in the city of Atlanta know his way around a set of woods without a guide, or map; just a flashlight.

Chapter Twenty-One
Netta

♩ Everybody plays the fool sometime
There's no exception to the rule
Listen, baby, it may be factual, may be cruel
I ain't lyin', everybody plays the fool
Falling in love is such an easy thing to do
And there's no guarantee that the one you love
Is gonna love you ♩

I was back at square one and hadn't laid eyes on Mason in months. My home began to deteriorate before my eyes until I was hit with an eviction notice, for failing to comply with the program rules to keep the utilities connected. Shortly after arriving home from the vacation from hell he had taken off with my rent money, the book of food stamps, and my car. He promised me that he would go and flip the money I had given him but the moment he didn't come home that night, I knew something wasn't right.

The morning after his disappearing act, I called every hospital, jail and morgue in the city, but no one had a body that belonged to Mason Vactor. He also didn't fit the description of any John Does. Shame kept me from reaching out to Ms. Arlene. I hadn't laid eyes on her since the day I picked up the kids. I stayed inside of the car with my ruined face and two black eyes, pretending to be drained and sleeping from the trip. Truth be told, I knew she would go ballistic when she saw all the new scars I'd gained over 72 hours. I didn't want to hear her tell me to leave; I didn't want to hear any more of her stories about similar situations. I just wanted to get my children and go home. So, I sat in the passenger seat of the car and I laid there with my eyes closed pretending to be sleep, while tears rolled down my face.

"Yes, ma'am I understand that. It's just that my kids and I don't have anywhere else to live. Please, I'll do anything; just don't take my home away from me!" I begged the leasing agent. I didn't care about pride; all I cared about was ending up right back on the streets of Atlanta during wintertime. My children were bundled up tight in their coats as Jack Frost unforgivingly, whipped around the downtown buildings.

"Ms. Bell, you know the qualifications of this program and I wish there was more that I could do, but the only thing I can do at this moment is put your file in front of management and let them decide if they want to re-enter you into the program with a different property. We have multiple properties and recipients, so I can't make any promises or give you a definite time frame, but I can give you my business card and you will have to reach out to me on a weekly basis to find out when a decision has been made." the agent said to me pitifully.

I wanted to make a scene, but I knew the only thing that would happen would be me getting tossed out of the building on my ass. I had nobody to blame but myself. I hadn't been to work since Mason left and I had ignored every attempt Ms. Arlene made to reach out to me. So, I used the little amount of dignity I had left to grab the hands of my two oldest children and to put my youngest child on my hip. I held my façade until I made it out of the door but the moment I was far enough away from the building to not be seen, I broke down. I fell to my knees as I screamed out for God to help me because I didn't know what else to do. I had nothing and no one. The only person that had shown me any piece of love, I turned my back on her.

Mason held his little sisters tightly as I cried, screamed,

My Mother's Man

and lost my mind on the sidewalk like a lunatic. I wished I could trade lives with someone at that moment. I wished I could just take my entire life and the mess I made of it, and hand it all off to another person. I sat homeless, hungry and defeated with my three children and two bags filled with clothing and toiletries.

"Mama, I'm hungry" Wayne cried.

"I know that, don't you think I am too, huh?! What you want me to do? Any ideas?" I asked my son angrily.

"We can go back to Mama Arl-" he tried to say before I cut him off.

"AHT, AHT, we can't go back there! That lady is sick and tired of us and she has the right to be; I can't even look her in her face right now! So, since you don't have any better suggestions, just sit there and stay in a child's place while I think." I told him.

He didn't say anything to make me angry enough to go off on him the way I did, I just felt like a terrible mother and there was nothing else I could do.

"No, Larry! What you don't understand is you told your daughter, actually promised her, that you would be In town for her birthday, so it doesn't matter what you buy, spend, or give, it won't be her father there!" I heard a familiar voice say.

The pretty brown skinned girl and the tall, skinny guy were walking in our direction. She looked so different, if I hadn't heard her speak, I wouldn't have known who she was. I thought I was dreaming, but I took my chances and called out my older sister's name anyway, because what did I have to lose if it wasn't her?

"Pearly Mae?!" I called out loud enough for her to hear me, but not loud enough to scare her and make a scene.

Her and the man both stopped and turned around. That was when I realized that I also knew the man she was with.; he was one of the men that frequented my mother's juke joint. Clearly My mother's customers had a thing for her daughters.

My big sister stopped and looked at me for a while. I knew that it had been around 10 years, but I knew I couldn't have looked that different from the last time she saw me.

"It's Netta, your little sister. Pearly Girl?" I asked her, calling her by her nick name. I was starting to get aggravated that the bitch was still acting like she didn't know me. "And you, I know you." I told him pointing, accusingly at the man. "You used to be at my mama's juke joint. You were a regular customer and I could never forget all the plates and drinks I fixed you. I know you recognize me!" I told him still hoping to be recognized, and not looked at like a crazy, homeless lady.

"Yeah, you Maddie's girl. Cook the hell out of some hog maws; look it's your little sister, baby!" he said clearly more excited to see me than my own flesh and blood. "How you been girl? These your kids?" He asked me, smiling big and showing all his teeth.

He looked like he wasn't old enough to be her father, but at least an older uncle. You could tell the way he grabbed her shoulders possessively that they were a couple. The one thing I couldn't deny was how good she looked; my big sister had my mother's slender figure and light complexion. Her hair was the biggest thing on her body and everything about her was so well coordinated, there was no denying that she was well taken care of. Even though she was yet another one of Maddie's daughters that had been preyed upon by one of her older customers, at least she'd gotten the good end of the deal and chosen a man that seemed to really care for her.

My sister still hadn't said a single word. She just looked at me in pity like I was a dirty homeless person begging her for change.

"Hey, Netta Boo." she said dryly as if it aggravated her to even say my name.

"How you been, sis?" I asked genuinely happy to see her, even if the love wasn't reciprocated.

"I been good, just taking care of these kids and the household, while this man works himself into an early grave to make sure his girls don't want or need for anything." she said looking at the man smiling.

"So how many kids do you have? How many nieces and nephews do I have?" I asked her.

She smiled the first genuine smile I saw since I'd bumped into her.

"Well, if my wonderful husband Jason could stop pulling so much overtime you could have been had a nephew, but you have 3 spoiled nieces. The oldest is 10, middle child is 8, youngest is turning 5. We have a nice house out in East Point, Georgia with 5 bedrooms and 5 bathrooms. I cooked a big dinner on Sunday; mama, Jean, Edith, Eddie, Randall, and Willa Mae all came over to house and ate!" she said nonchalantly, as if she hadn't just told me that pretty much my entire family had dinner without me.

"Oh ok, that sounds good. What about John and Laverne, why didn't they show up to the big family feast?" I asked her, trying to hide my anger.

"Well, John has been in prison for about 3 years and Laverne has been on crack for so long, we don't even bother keeping track of her." she said waving her hand dismissively.

My heart dropped. I hoped my sister was ok.

"And who are these beautiful big kids right here?" Jason asked looking down at my babies smiling.

"Well, these are your nieces and your nephew." I said looking directly at Pearly Mae. "This is the oldest and my only son, Mason; he is 8 years old about to be 9." I said pointing at a now smiling Mason.

"Mason, this is your auntie Pearl and your uncle Jason." I told him glad that Pearly had said her husband's name, because I never knew it.

"Hey auntie, hey uncle!" he said waving excitedly.

It was the first smile I'd saw on his face in all day and it warmed my heart. I know it must have felt good to meet someone that I introduced them to besides Ms. Arlene.

"These are your two nieces; this is Terri she's 5, and this is Bonnie she's three!" I said pointing at my two younger girls who waved, but were too tired, hungry, and aggravated to put on a fake smile like their older brother.

"Hello girls!" my sister said in a tone that sounded forced and a smile too wide to be authentic.

"Well, it was nice to chat with y'all. I'm going to get home and cook for these girls before they get out of school." my sister said while grabbing her husband's hand, trying to pull him in the opposite direction.

"Wait, hold on baby. What y'all doing out here? Waiting for a ride? We can shoot y'all home." Jason offered. "As a matter of fact, how about y'all come over for dinner, then we can take y'all home later. Your sister can throw down in the kitchen, y'all get that from your mama. Besides, Y'all aint seen each other in years, y'all need to do more catching up besides this little dry stranger talk. Come on, I parked close by here. These y'all bags?" he asked as he grabbed one of the bags from Wayne and the other from me.

"No, we're fine." I started before my sister rushed in.

"Baby, she said they're fine, give them back their bags let's go." she said looking him eye to eye, as if she was trying to throw a hint that she prayed he would catch.

I felt terrible. In that moment; I felt like I was no better in her eyes than my sister Laverne she had just called a crack head and dismissed.

"Yeah, don't get into trouble brother in law, listen to your wife." I said smiling at him, appreciating what he was trying to do while reaching to take my bags back.

I wished I had kept my mouth shut and let my big sister walk on by, it would have been a better feeling than feeling like worthless trash. A blind man could see that me and my children weren't in the best shape. It was freezing outside, my kids were bundled up, and they looked uncomfortable, we also had big bags. What decent mother would have her children out here if she didn't have to? Hell, what decent mother would be on the side of the street that type of day if she wasn't picking up dinner or headed home from work? I could see on my sister's face that she wasn't oblivious to what was going on. She knew something wasn't right, she just didn't care.

"Nonsense, ain't nobody getting in trouble, this family right here." Jason said taking the bags and heading off towards the car with Wayne on his heels. I stood and looked at my sister awkwardly. She looked at me then my girls, before turning to follow her husband, without another word. We followed her.

Chapter Twenty-Two
Netta

When we pulled up to my sister's driveway, I realized she wasn't lying about their house. It was a beautiful home and reminded me of a slightly larger version of Mason's old home. Unlike Mason's old home that looked like a bachelor pad, imitating a family home, this house looked like it was a family home.

On the outskirts of East Point, GA in a nice suburban neighborhood; my big sister's home nestled comfortably on the row of houses. When we pulled into the driveway, the first thing I noticed was her large front yard; it was a good yard for a nice big family BBQ. I wondered not if, but how many big BBQ's she'd hosted that my siblings, mother, and her friends had shown up to. I didn't dwell on the thought because it hurt too much to think about.

"I got the bags, ladies. Y'all go on up and get y'all a little some to sip on. Make yourself at home, little sis." Jason said smiling at my sister and I, as we walked up the driveway into the house.

He clearly adored my sister. I wondered if it was genuine or if he was putting on an act, like Mason did to make me feel like he was a good man. Before the night was out, I would know the answer to my own question. One thing I learned from Mason that I didn't admit to myself until a few years in was, even when he was being nice, the red flags had always been there. I just looked over them because I felt like the good qualities outweighed the bad. That was until his bad continued to show itself more and more with each passing day. Soon his true colors completely overshadowed all the things that were fake about him.

"Yeah, bring that stuff in and you better hurry up before we drink all my wine and raid your liquor cabinet!" she yelled over her shoulder jokingly.

I looked back to catch his facial expression. He was smiling at her comment and his expression told me that he didn't care what she raided, as long as she was happy. Right then and there, I knew that I had been chosen by the wrong older man from my mother's juke joint.

"Take off y'all shoes at the door. When my husband brings in the bags he'll leave em at the door automatically, so I can wash whatever y'all have in them. He knows I don't play that nasty shit in my house!" my sister said as soon as we made it inside of the door. I don't think my kids cared what was said or done to them, they were happy to just be inside of a heated home and out of the cold winter air.

"Take off y'all coats and I'll give you a clothes hanger to hang them on in the coat closet. We don't keep everything anywhere here; we have order in this house." she said not to them but at them, as if they weren't used to a clean home with order.

I watched Wayne remove his coat and put it on the clothes hanger his aunt handed him, before removing both of his sister's coats and repeating the same process. I wanted to curse her ass out, but I felt just as good as the kids to see a familiar face and to be in a warm home.

The sitting room was sparsely decorated with one grey sectional and a large multicolored rug underneath. There was a wooden end table in front of the couch, and two more end tables on the opposite sides of the couch. There was a tall lamp turned on and the large window that was covered with long grey drapes. The kitchen held a grey island in the center, and it was very large.

"Let me take you on a quick tour." my sister said smiling genuinely. I could tell she loved her home and showed it off every chance she got.

"This is me and my husband's room," she said while showing me the master bedroom that was easily the size of my apartment. Their huge bed sat on a step that made the room look multilayered; similar to Mason's home. The bedroom had a large walk out patio, adorned with patio furniture. The bedroom furniture was wooden and gave off a decorated cabin in the woods feel, with all the soft earth tones she used to decorate. The fireplace crackled in the corner and she walked over to it and used the metal stick to move the wood around. Their bathroom was large also and a jacuzzi styled tub just big enough for two, sat in the middle of the large bathroom. The tub sat next to a window that I'm sure overlooked the back yard.

There was a room used for guest, and the girls each had their own bedroom. The dining room held a large table with 5 chairs, and she had an enormous basement, as well as a really, big back yard. Her basement was decorated and used as an entertainment room; It was a perfect home to raise a family.

"Your home is beautiful, sis!" I told her genuinely impressed. Their home was clean, decorated perfectly, spacious, and so very cozy. As the girls played together and my son watched tv while waiting for dinner, my sister and I stood in the kitchen sipping wine and talking.

"Thank you, it's all because of Jason. I can't lie, he is a hell of a man. He has been spoiling me since we got together. The minute we found out I was pregnant with our first daughter, he married me. He told me that he wanted me and his kids to have his last name and he promised me that he would spend the rest of his life proving to me that I had made the right choice with picking him. He hasn't broken his promise. He is a truck driver and he makes sure that his daughters, and I have this lifestyle." she said, while stirring her green beans and sipping her wine.

"We don't want or need for anything; my biggest complaint is him spending more time home."

"Yeah, y'all are blessed." I said to her looking at the irony of the situation.

Before her and Jason walked by, I wished that I could trade lives with someone and then I run into one of my big sisters, that I haven't laid eyes on in years and she has the perfect life.

"So, how has mama and everyone been doing?" I asked her to try and change the subject.

"Mama is good, she finally let that juke joint go a little bit after you ran off with her man." she said, giving me the side eye while stirring her mashed potatoes. "As your big sister I just want you to know that, that shit was dead ass wrong, Netta. Mama was really in love with Mason and you hurt her. She couldn't eat, sleep, or do anything. Jean had to take care of our little brothers and sisters while she worked through all that emotional stress!" she told me looking me deep into my eyes and placing one hand on her slender hip, while reaching for her wine glass with the other.

"First off, did she tell you what happened? Hell, did any of them tell you what happened?" I asked her angrily.

It was just like my mother to play the victim and make me out to be a home wrecker. It was also just like my spineless ass siblings to not correct her, and let her drag my name through the mud. The same siblings I had cared for and was more of a mother to than she was! I couldn't expect Willa Mae or Randal to stand up for me because they were the youngest, but Jean was my twin brother; we were in the womb together! Where the hell was his sympathy for me? Edith and Eddie were old enough to see what the hell was going on, why didn't they defend me in my absence?

"It really doesn't matter what happened, Net. Out of all the men that came through that house, you want to fuck behind your own mother? How nasty is that? It's trifling and disgusting!" she said looking down her nose at me, like it was my intentions to land on the lap of my mother's man. As if I hadn't paid for my mistake repeatedly.

"You know what, big sis? I agree." I told her. "What I did wasn't right. I did it out of spite just to hurt mama and it ended up biting me in my ass. Landed me with two extra kids, by a cripple ass daddy that goes months without seeing them, takes food from their mouth, and a roof from over their heads. Mason has abused me in every way you could think of. He has tortured me and my children, caused me to try to commit suicide, caused me to lose EVERYTHING I have worked for! Thanks to him I'm jobless, homeless, carless, and I have nothing. He damages every woman he comes in contact with; It would have been more revenge for me to leave the nigga under mama's roof. I saved her ass and ruined my entire life! She should be thanking me. So, you or anyone else don't have to punish me for the foul move I made. Every day I wake up is punishment enough!" I told her with tears filling my eyes. For the first time I admitted to myself as well as someone else, that I'd played myself by giving myself to Mason.

"But even still, what I can't allow you to do is paint me as this trashy ass, homewrecker, that wanted to be in my mother's shoes so bad, that I just swooped up and stole her man! I was raped Pearly Mae, and you know what mother told me when I came to her crying?" I asked her getting closer. "She said take your bloody ass upstairs you ain't been raped, you gave it up to some young boy and got played." I revealed to my big sister.

"Well, it's just because she was raped too when she was younger, and our grandma didn't believe her either and-"

"Damn that, Pearl!" I told her throwing my hand up dismissing her sentence. "How long are we going to make excuses by saying because it was done to her, it was acceptable for her to do it to us? Huh?! If one of your girls came to you crying saying she had been taken advantage of, wouldn't you move heaven and hell to make sure she was ok? To put your foot up the ass of whoever hurt her? Make sure she felt safe again?!"

"Hell yes, without a doubt!"

"SO, WOULD I! Despite what I have been through I wouldn't do my daughters how mama did me. At some point you must call a spade a spade, and a toxic person a toxic person."

I told her wiping the tears from my eyes, downing the rest of my glass of wine in one gulp.

"MOMMY, MOMMY!!!!" my three nieces yelled as they ran into the house with their father behind them. I reflected on the days when my baby was doing the same, using his foot to kick the front door closed.

Chapter Twenty-Three
Netta

"That was good as hell, baby." My sister's husband said leaning back as far as the chair would allow, while rubbing his stomach, and looking at his wife adoringly. "Lady, I get the way to a man's heart is through his stomach; but if you don't stop going through my stomach with all these amazing meals my heart is going to bust from loving you so much."

"First of all, I love you more!" she said while gazing at him lovingly. "Secondly, Language. Good as *heck* would have been more child appropriate." she said glaring at him.

"My bad!" he said laughing and placing his hand over his mouth.

"Nope, daddy, a dollar for the jar!" his oldest daughter, Jade, said.

My sister's oldest daughter was a sassy little thing. She looked as well kept as her other sisters, but I could tell that she was spoiled rotten. My sister would have to break her from that because once a child starts to feel that you owe them a certain type of treatment, they will cut a fool if that treatment stops for whatever reason.

"You're right my princess, and daddy will put a dollar in the jar and work on his language." Jason said reaching into his pants pocket and pulling out a dollar to hand to his daughter. "Now, take your sisters and little cousins and go to your room. Mommy, daddy, and Auntie Netta, have some grown folks' things to discuss." he said looking at me, then at my sister seriously.

Me and my sister had never finished our conversation because she jumped into mommy mode when her babies made it home from school. I could tell she was a terrific mother, and her girls adored her as much as her husband did. However, the tension was so thick when we sat down to eat the Stringbeans with mashed potatoes, Pot Roast, Cornbread, and the homemade Peach Cobbler for dessert; that it could be cut with the same knife we were using to slice the Roast.

I kissed my son on his chocolate colored forehead, as he collected his two sisters and headed to the back of the house. I reached for another glass of wine before Jason placed his hand on top of mine gently, as if to say slow down on the alcohol. When I looked into his eyes, I knew that the touch wasn't in a sexual way but, more of a caring, brotherly way. Appreciating his genuine kindness, I reached for the glass of water instead. I prayed that my sister knew how blessed she was to have such a sweet man as a husband.

"Ok ladies, the tension is almost too thick to breathe through, so put it on the table like adults." he said placing his folded hands underneath his chin and looking from my sister to me, like a school guidance counselor.

"There is no tension, I understand that Netta has been having it hard, but like mama always says, once you make your bed, you must lie in it." Pearly Mae said dismissively taking a sip of her water. "Are you ready for my husband and I to drop you, the kids, and your bags off wherever you need to go?" she asked nonchalantly.

"Netta, I love my wife and sometimes she can be incredibly stubborn." Jason said looking at me and cutting his eye at Pearl. "You and the kids aren't going anywhere."

"What do you mean Jason? this is my house."

"This is, **OUR**, house. This house belongs to both you and your husband and your husband doesn't turn his back on family. I wasn't raised like that and you know it!" he said looking at her.

I felt terrible being the cause of their argument, but a small part of me felt good because it had been so long since I had someone to care about my children and I; and be on our side.

"Don't argue because of me. I don't have to be anywhere that I'm not welcomed, so I will grab my kids and you can just take us back where you got us, Pearl. I don't cause trouble and despite what lies you have been told about me, I'm not a bad person. I would think that you were aware of that, you lived in the same house with me until you were 18 years old!"

"Yeah, but my sweet, little sister, would never do some of the shit I've been hearing out here. The streets are loud baby girl and I don't live in them, but I have friends. I hear about how you out here fighting for Mason, approaching women about him, catching and passing all kinds of nasty diseases. You can actually take those dishes you and your kids were eating out of with you." she said with disgust.

"I'm not one to disrespect a person in their house, so let me get the fuck up out your house before I tell you some real disrespectful things. Also make sure you check your sources really, good because I don't sleep around. I have been with two men my entire life honey, TWO!" I said to her holding up my two fingers in her face. "Only one of them was voluntary! The only thing I'm guilty of is being in love with a low-down man. Mason got me jumped on in front of my children, he is the one out here messing with all these women and passing stuff out. He is the reason I'm homeless right now with no job, No car, no money; while you are sitting on your high horse, make sure you thank whoever is sitting up there and looking down for the man you have. I'm a living testimony that loving the wrong person can destroy your entire damn life! Thank you for the meal and for washing our clothes." I told her while scooting back from the table and heading to grab my children. I had no idea where we would go, but as long as I had them and they had me, we could be in a damn cardboard box for all I cared.

"WAIT! You sit down and you," Jason said turning to his wife. "Out of all the things I have told you about my past, growing up with nothing and nobody until someone came along and showed me some kindness, you would really be this heartless and let your little sister and her small children walk outside of this door with nowhere to turn?!" he asked her in disbelief.

"Baby liste-" she started before he cut her off.

"No, forget all that! I don't care what she has or hasn't done. I'm from the streets, I ran with cats like Mayday. He's a Pretty boy that gets any woman he wants, and he uses and abuses them. Just so happen that he came in between a mother and daughter's relationship that was already walking on a fine line as it was, and he used it to his advantage!"

"That's what the hell I have been trying to tell her Jason, but no one wants to listen to me!" I said finally relieved that someone understood. "Me and mama's relationship was already destroyed, Pearl! He was there the night I came home when I got raped, he was there when me and mommy argued, he knew that I wanted out of that situation; that house, that life, and that I would take the first exit I saw. He pretended to care for me and offered me an exit. I just didn't know that the exit would be the worst decision I would ever make in my life." I told her walking around to her side of the table, so that I could be face to face with my sister. Even if she didn't let me and my kids live in her home, I wanted her to understand that I wasn't a monster; I was still Netta, her little sister.

"I understand that. So how about this, I can just give you and the kids a couple of days but I know the girls won't like this. They like having their own room and, their own space but like my husband said your family, so it's ok." she said clearly, only giving in so she wouldn't have to fight with her husband.

Part of me wanted to tell her to shove her offer up her ass, but I heard the wind whistling off the trees and I knew that Jack Frost was directing traffic outside. I knew it was too cold for my babies to be outside with their thin coats. We would probably have walking pneumonia by daybreak. They needed to be in a warm home, in a warm cozy bed. So, I bit my tongue and accepted the bullshit offer for a warm place to sleep.

"Thank you, sis and thank you brother in law. Me and the kids appreciate it, and I'm sorry for putting my little nieces out of their rooms. It will only be for a short little while." I said while picking up the plates from the table to clear it.

"You don't have to do that; you are a guest." Jason said.

"No please, let me do this. I just want to show you guys my appreciation because you didn't have to open your door to me and the kids. Just let me show you how much I appreciate it." I said looking at my big sister eye to eye.

She broke my gaze to look down at her shirt as if she was brushing something away, but I knew it was just the guilt; there was nothing there to brush away. She was just as flawless as she had been all day.

A couple of days turned into a couple of months as my sister and I mended our relationship. She and her husband helped me until I got back on my feet, proving to me that God really did answer prayers. I just wished he would answer my prayer to cleanse my addiction to Mason. When I ran back into him at The Varsity, while grabbing my babies something to eat, I invited him to come over and see his daughters after he begged me for an hour and a half.

Home was now a little efficiency apartment, that my sister and brother in law helped me get and furnish for me and the kids. After he played with his daughters for 15 minutes, ate the hot meal I prepared for the kids, and made love to me that night, I realized that I was yet again doing the same thing, with the same man, hoping that the outcome would be different. Einstein defined it as insanity.

Chapter Twenty-Four
Netta

"I understand that you have to pay the rent and put food in the house, baby but ima take the money and these food stamp dollars and bring back way more. When I get done, we going to have enough to pay the rent, fill the box with groceries for 3 months, buy you a new car, and take the kids to Disney World. My babies need a vacation!" Mason told me over dinner.

"Mayday, it's too soon for you to go out and work again." I told him across the dinner table.

I had cooked all his favorites and we were having our nightly, family discussion. The smothered Oxtails, white rice, pinto beans, and cornbread plate I made him, hadn't been touched while me and the kids were chowing down on the feast. I knew something was on his mind, but I didn't press him to tell me. I just asked Wayne about his day and made idle play talk with the kids, until he was ready to tell me what was on his mind.

"Mayday, I trust your business and I know that you can do whatever you put your mind to, I have witnessed you at the top of your game. Business was booming, you had the flyest whips, nicest clothes, and you put me up in that huge ass house of yours because of your work ethic. All im saying is that for one, the money that I have on me is for bills and for two,"

"FUCK FOR TWO!" he screamed jumping up from the table. "You like having a brother in this position. Tables done turned a lil bit and you like the fact that you control the purse!" He said picking up his plate of food and throwing it in my direction.

The plate crashed into the kitchen counter and all the food sprawled all over the table, hitting me and the kids. Terri and Bonnie began to cry; Wayne didn't shed a tear or even move a muscle, he just stared straight forward, not looking to Mason or at me.

"Now Mason, was that really called for?" I asked him while wiping food from my face and shirt calmly. I stood to go to the kitchen to grab the rag to clean up the mess he'd made. I tried to remain calm so the situation wouldn't blow up further.

"Wayne, get your sisters and go to your room." I said while wetting the dish rag.

"Naw, everybody going to stay right where I can see them!" he said. "I don't trust his police calling ass as far as I can throw him!" he said pointing at Wayne.

"Real men don't run to the law, they handle things themselves, little boy!" he said to Wayne as if he didn't switch on Clara and sing like a canary when the officer walked in.

"The kids are tired; they don't have to see this!"

Mason was across the table and on my ass before I could complete my sentence. Even without full use of both of his legs, he was strong as hell. He straddled my waist and used everything he could grab within arm's reach to hit me in my face, until I raised my arms to catch the blows. Attempting to block his hits must have aggravated him because it went from bad, to worse. The cutting board I had just used to cut up all the vegetables for dinner banged my elbows

"Naw move your arms, you done got above yourself! Bitch get a lil car, a lil apartment, learn how to read a few three letter words, and start smelling her ass! MOVE, YOUR DAMN ARMS OUT THE WAY" he screamed out as he continued to hit my forearms and elbows, attempting to get to my face.

"I got some for you." he said before opening the kitchen

drawer and taking out a hammer. He banged my forearms with the metal hammer like they were nails that he couldn't get into a cement wall.

All I could do was scream and try to protect my face and head while switching from arm to arm to alternate the pain. I wasn't sure how much more I could take because I was sure the bones in both forearms had to be shattered. My arms involuntarily fell to my sides leaving my face and head exposed, and I knew that I wouldn't make it out alive. So, instead of looking Mason eye to eye, I did what I'm sure any mother would do If she had the opportunity to look at her babies one last time. I turned to face them sitting at the kitchen table crying and told them I loved them before I felt the worse pain I'd ever felt in my life.

The hammer crashed into the side of my face instantly caving it in, as I felt my teeth detach from my gums and fall to the opposite side of my mouth. Everything in me wanted to raise my arms but they were too heavy and now my head felt heavy as well. There was no fight left inside of me as I felt him continue to hit me with the hammer, until I no longer felt anything else.

Chapter Twenty-Five
Mason

"And like I told you my brother, violence is never the answer; take it from someone who ain't never going to see the light of day again." I told my young cell mate.

It was the year 2019, and I'd been in Jackson State prison serving a life sentence for killing the mother of my children; for 20 years. I didn't know why I continued to keep track of time because I was never going to get out of here.

"Listen old school, I hear ya but check it; it's just that things have changed since you been free. We in a new time period, May Day!" the youngin said to me.

His name was Tony Wright, but he went by the nickname Amazin; he told me it was his rap name. I didn't understand why all these little young boys wanted to be rappers. He couldn't have been more than 120 pounds soaking wet. He stood around 6 feet tall, and every inch of his body was marked with tattoos. Surprisingly his face was uncovered; well except for a scar in the middle of his forehead. However, what he lacked in weight he made up for with heart. Since he was transferred from Autry State Prison, he had been taking niggas heads off that came at him wrong. Even though he was 5 years into a 10-year bid for armed robbery, he made it clear that he would die for his respect and because of that he had my respect.

"Y'all lil young boys kill me wit that different time shit." I told him waving my hand dismissively. "You know history don't do nothing but repeat itself right? So, everything y'all young cats even thinking of doing, we done did it and wrote the book on it. We were wearing them tight ass pants in the 70's that y'all wearing now, mackin on hoes, shooting the breeze, dipping in and out of cat holes; that shit ain't new whipper snapper!" I told him laughing.

Whenever we were sitting around getting high this new school versus old school debate would come up, and I was tired of schooling this young twenty something fool, who thought he knew everything.

"Look man first off, what the hell is a shooting a breeze, huh? The only thing we shoot around here besides a nigga, is our shot with a bad lil vibe; you need to catch this wave, Unk." he told me laughing. "Then what the fuck is a whipper snapper? Is that a type of fish or some? Cause to keep it a hunnid, I don't fuck with all different types of fish, I like Tilapia and whiting every now and then." he said looking serious. I put my forehead in my hands. He didn't understand nothing I said and I damn sure didn't understand what he meant by a vibe and a wave.

"But look O.G., you need to let me put you down because if I drip some of this young nigga swag on you, you going to be the coldest 61-year-old in this mufucka."

"PUT A LID ON IT MAYDAY!" the guard yelled through my door.

To the average ear you would have thought he was telling me to keep my voice down or shut up, but he was really letting me know to put my weed out because they were on their way to do count. When I came to prison at the tender age of 36, I knew I would be in here for the rest of my life. So, I did what all lifers do, I made myself at home. I made connections, friends that turned into family, and I turned to Jesus for forgiveness for all the sins I'd committed. I had more peace in my life in the 25 years I had been in prison, than my 36 years being a free man. I knew that everything I had been through was all a part of God's divine plan. I attended bible study for inmates and church every Sunday, volunteered whenever I could, and used all my free time to preach to any young boy that would listen, to try not to get him to make the same mistakes I did.

Putting out the dooby and putting it in my secret place, I fanned my clothes to try to get rid of some of the smell on me. Reaching my arms high over my head to stretch while I yawned, I scratched just above my shoulder blade and my fingers grazed my scar. It was the scar from the knife that Wayne put into my shoulder the night I'd beat his mother's face into a bloody pulp.

It was the knife in my shoulder that brought me back to reality. I zoned out as I continued to smash her skull in with the hammer, long after her lifeless body had stopped moving. It wasn't until I came out of my trance, that I realized what I had done.

For the first five years of my sentence, every time I closed my eyes, I saw her once beautiful black, porcelain face smashed in like a stepped-on porcelain doll. Her brain fragments were all over the floor and chunky like salsa, I smelled the urine as well as her last bowel movement. The smell as well as the scene before me caused me to dry heave.

Reaching around to touch the place where the terrible stinging came from, standing directly behind me, was Wayne. I watched him grow up, so I was sure his eyes were hazel. However, as if he had on colored contacts, his once hazel eyes were replaced with a black color, as dark as charcoal. As quickly as he put the knife in my back the first time, he snatched it out with the strength and speed that surpassed his 9 years and was about to plunge it in again before he heard

FREEZE. POLICE.

I wasn't sure when he called the police, but there I was red handed with a bloody hammer in my hand, straddling a woman with a crushed face. It was a no brainer that I would receive life, plus 20 years without the possibility of parole. As I was handcuffed and walking past my crying daughters, I took a good mental picture, because I knew I would never see them again.

"Now, that sound like some sissified shit boy. What the hell is, put me down and drip on me? The only niggas that's getting put down and dripped on in here is niggas that's washing other niggas draws." I told him. "Y'all be listening to this crazy ass music like the lil black boy that's on the country song; you know us niggas ain't meant to be on no country music. Now y'all young minds screwed up because it ain't no black men in the homes. They all in here; or at Phillips, Autry, Baldwin, the list goes on and on. So, who our lil black boys got as role models? Lil black, gay rappers talking about whipping horses, niggas wearing dresses, and rappers persuading them to do shit they own kids ain't doing. They out here telling your kids to rob, steal, and kill while their kids are in the private schools with the other rich, trust fund kids. Then all y'all wanna be rappers. No disrespect to your dream young boy, but if everybody a rapper who the hell going to build these million-dollar mansions y'all buying?" I told him trying to put the boy on game.

Before he could respond we heard, "LINE UP!"

The C.O yelled out his nightly mantra as if we didn't see him at the same time, in this same place, for the same reason, every damn night. I gave him the worst mug I could create. Despite my initial efforts to put the cool Mayday charm on him to get in his good graces, like I had done all the other prison officials. He was determined not to like me. He was a tall, high yellow, pretty boy that was as country as me; everyone said he was a police officer before he switched to corrections.

"Peddle Way, I didn't get a chance to get my meds, so I need to go to the infirmary before lights out." one of the other inmates told him.

"Ok, no problem, but next time your ass needs to remember." he said giving the inmate a hard time, still being kind towards him.

Everyone loved officer Peddle Way because he treated inmates like people and not animals. Well, everyone except me.

My Mother's Man

He had been at this prison facility for 10 of the 25 years I had been here, and even though I never met him, he'd made my life a living hell from the very beginning. Every attempt he made to sabotage me didn't go as planned because I had a 15-year head start there. Anyone he tried to turn against me already liked me too much. It was one of the rare cases where, the officers stood with an inmate, over their fellow law enforcement brother. His vendetta against me only made enemies for him, and it made me laugh in his face every time I saw him.

"BACK THE FUCK UP AND LET YOUR BACK TOUCH THE BARS! AINT NO TIME FOR ALL THIS CHIT CHAT!" Peddle Way said, yelling out loud but looking directly at me.

I smiled my crooked smile at him and limped backwards like he asked. I looked him eye to eye maliciously as my full smile turned into a sly smirk, I was too blessed to be stressed.

Chapter Twenty-Six
Mason

"Get your ass up! Chow is over for you; I need you on clean up detail!" C.O Peddle Way said to me even though I'd just sat down to eat, and he knew it.

I was sick of this nigga fucking with me, so I was about to put some plans into place to make this nigga as uncomfortable as he was trying to make me. I didn't need other people thinking it was cool to try me because of him.

"I'M TALKING TO YOU INMATE, GET UP NOW!" he screamed over me, letting his spit fly into my meatloaf and mashed potatoes.

The chow hall went quiet. All eyes were on me as niggas chewed their food, waiting for my reaction; they loved a show. I jumped up as fast as one real and fake leg would allow, grabbed my food tray with both hands, and slammed it across the officer's yellow face. The entire chow hall became chaotic as inmates began to whoop and holler. Other officers rushed over and began speaking into their walkie talkies for back up.

Being shocked from the impact but immediately regaining control, officer Peddle Way took his stick from his belt and hit me across my face repeatedly. The blows were coming so quick I didn't have time to dodge them. I hadn't made it in prison this long being a punk nigga, so I continued to fight giving it all I had. I was in terrific shape but still, I was too old for this shit; my fighting days were long behind me.

Before I could continue to throw blows, I felt multiple hands take hold of me; it was the other officers swooping in to defend their own. He continued to beat me for longer than he had to before Officer Reynolds yelled out "ENOUGH, Peddle Way!" I smiled through my bloody lips.

"BUT NO ONE WAS THERE TO YELL OUT ENOUGH FOR, NETTA THOUGH; PUNK MOTHERFUCKER! YOU BEAT HER TO DEATH WITH A HAMMER, IN FRONT OF HER FUCKIN KIDS! TODAY MAKES 25 YEARS, YOU NO LEG HAVING SON OF A BITCH!" he screamed in my face as spit from his lips slapped into my face.

With every ounce of disrespect, he then gathered up enough spit to put out a forest fire and, spit directly into my face. He then walked away angrily, looking emotionally wrecked. I didn't know how he knew Netta and I didn't really give a shit, because I had forgiven myself for killing her a long time ago.

However, at that moment, I mentally signed his death certificate. I didn't have shit to lose and I would be damned if a nigga would come and disrupt the only home I would ever have for the rest of my time on this earth.

Wayne Bell

"Your mother would be rolling in her grave if she could see you right now, Wayne." Ms. Arlene told me. She still had the thin frame I'd known from my childhood; the only difference was my 200 pound 6'2 frame now towered over hers. "Where did I go wrong with you boy?" she asked me over the telephone disappointed. I could see the tears fill her eyes and watch her facial expression through the glass partition that separated us.

"I watched my father kill my mother; I was doomed from the start." I told her nonchalantly but truthfully.

It hurt me to hurt her so much. She had done an amazing job with my two little sisters. Terri was happily married, working for the State of Georgia, and expecting her second child, which would be my first nephew any day now. My niece whom she named Jeanette after our mother, was a three-year-old; little chocolate drop of love and energy. She loved to color and draw. Every over the line colored, or poorly drawn picture she had ever created for Uncle Wayne, graced whatever cell I occupied. I would die and go to hell for the women in my family; many niggas wound up hurt for touching my niece's drawings on my wall.

Bonnie was an airman in the Air Force. She didn't want to get married and have kids just yet; instead she travelled all around this big beautiful world and constantly brought home souvenirs and gifts. I was the only screw up. Ms. Arlene didn't tell me frequently, but I could always tell by her facial expression whenever I disappointed her. She gave me and my sisters an amazing home. She loved, nurtured, and protected us better

My Mother's Man

than our own mother did. She truly was a blessing from God. That was why I couldn't tell her that this was all part of my plan.

Every juvenile stint, that turned into a jail stint, that prepared me for minor prison stints, were all a part of my plan to spend the rest of my life in prison because I knew that after I took Mason's life, I would never see the outside of a prison again and I was mentally prepared for that. I would never forget, nor would I forgive the man that brutally took my birth mother's life. There wasn't a day that passed that I didn't have nightmares about that night. I simply grew older and stopped complaining about the dreams. Therapy didn't help because I didn't want it to. Sex didn't help, money didn't help; I never allowed myself to love a woman on a relationship level because I didn't want to grow attached and leave her; either my father would kill me, or I would kill him. The earth wasn't big enough for us both. I prayed every night for God to protect him until I made it to him.

"I know you don't understand," I started before she cut me off.

"Oh, but I do. I have taken care of you since you were 7 years old, Wayne. I know that your mother's death took a bigger toll on you than it did on your sisters; That was why I gave you extra love and care. To this day they joke that you are the favorite, but they don't understand that you went through the most. I thought I could love you past your terrible childhood." she told me.

"I know you better than you know yourself and I know the dreams never stopped coming, you just stopped coming into my room to crawl into bed with me. I used to hold you, and soothe your young broken heart. I know that you started to get into trouble because you are praying that you're going to wind up in one of these prisons with Mayday's trashy ass, so you can get revenge on him for what he did to Netta. I just always prayed that eventually you would forgive him, not for him but for yourself, so you could enjoy your life, get married, have kids of your own, travel the world. I don't support you throwing your life away for revenge, but I will love you and your sisters until I take my very last breath." she told me while standing up and placing the phone back in its cradle.

I put my outstretched hand on the glass separating us and she put her hand in the same place, on the opposite side of the glass. She may have known more than I thought she did but she didn't know that I was transferring prison's the next day and going to Autry State, to avenge my mother's death.

I didn't have a life to enjoy, because it was taken from me the day that bastard killed my mother.

Chapter Twenty-Seven
<u>Mason</u>

♪Revenge
I'll cut your throat
I'll make amends
Ha! Ha!
I'm mad
That's a fact
Get ready, dog
For the big payback ♪

  I had been in the hole for 3 months since my chow hall brawl with the corrections officer. Even though I had connections, it was the minimum standard punishment for assaulting any officer, no matter how small or big the assault. It didn't matter to me though. My solitude only gave me more quiet time to plan my revenge. Officer Peddle Way received a minor love tap, only getting suspended for two weeks for spitting in my face. It angered me even more thinking about how no matter how hard a nigga tried to change his ways, trouble always seemed to follow and lurk around corners like a damn rapist in a van.

  My resources kept me up to date on everything that went on in the general population during my brief absence. Like I said, I had a 15-year head start on my officer rival, and my relationships were solidified. I knew that my cellmate Tony had been transferred to another prison after a big altercation in the yard, so another man had been occupying my cell for a month and a half. I hope that nigga hadn't touched my pictures or magazines. That current cell had been my home for 12 years, so I was as protective of it, as a person would be towards their apartment.

I heard this new guy was a petty criminal. He was slightly older than Tony but unlike Tony, he was seasoned. He had a few allies because he was no stranger to the system. I was told that he was only doing a few years for something minor. I felt that maybe I could talk some sense into him, and try to teach him somethings, to keep him from behind these walls. That was until Officer Reynolds informed me that he had become close to Officer Peddle Way. I began to include him in my plan and I planned to make the young nigga's life hell, just to get to the officer. He had nothing to do with this decade long beef but it was a dirty game, and sometimes the good had to suffer with the bad.

Aggravated was an understatement of how I felt when I stepped into my cell and noticed the changes. Instead of my bible scriptures, pictures of naked women, and beautiful places I liked to imagine I was visiting whenever I was angry, the pictures had been replaced with a bunch of childlike colored pages and drawings. This nigga must have lost his mind. I immediately began snatching the pictures down, while ripping them in the process, throwing them on the ground. I tried to leave my past ways behind me but clearly, I had to reintroduce myself.

After putting all MY things back on MY walls, I settled down to relax and have a smoke of some good weed, before it was time to go to chow. Searching in my secret hiding space inside of my mattress for my weed, I was angry when I didn't feel it there. Did that motherfucker Tony get me before he got transferred because he knew the chances were slim of us ever bumping back into each other? The new nigga didn't know about my stash and the guards would never search that spot because they already knew that was where I kept my weed.

"It had to be Tony!" I said to myself aloud before I heard the cell door open.

"I want you to take care of yourself." Peddle Way said as he led the young man inside of my cell.

The first thing I noticed about him besides his large frame and heavily muscled physique, was his eyes. They were dark and lifeless, reminding me of that crazy, cracker cult leader, from the late 60's, Charles Manson. He had a low haircut and the most perfect chocolate complexion I'd ever laid eyes on.

"What's up Pops?" he asked me smiling; holding his hands up like we were long lost friends. "That weed you had was the good shit, your old cellie Tony told me all about it before his little accident." He said smirking at me, letting me know that he had something to do with whatever happened to Tony.

"First of all, little nigga, I ain't your Pops! I don't have a son; I have two beautiful baby girls but that's it; ain't no nigga came out these nuts!" I told him while grabbing my dick and mugging him disrespectfully. I was going to have to teach this little nigga some manners. "I got a few hoes I used to knock down back in the day though, so what bitch done lied to you and told you I was ya pappy?" I said smiling at Peddle Way, still not knowing who the young nigga was.

"Well, it's been a few years, so let me properly introduce you two. Wayne Bell, Mason Vactor. Mason Vactor this is Wayne Bell." Officer Peddle Way said smiling, waiting for the look on my face when I'd realized that I was in a cell with my son; The son I'd shared with the woman whose life I'd took. I couldn't do shit but smile.

"Oh ok, yeah. I knew you looked like this rapist I knew back in the day." I said laughing and folding my arms across my chest, while widening my stance. "I thought that old bitch, Arlene, told you since she hates my guts. Then again, maybe your mama never told her. When we got together you were one year's old. She was raped one night while she delivered food and liquor for her mother. So yeah, you a rape baby, son. I don't know if you remember this," I snickered before continuing. "but I used to tease you all the time and say get your hands off my daughters you little rapist, you going to grow up exactly like your daddy and be a rapist. Is that what you in here for now?" I asked with a smirk on my face. "I can't wait till I tell the boys this, you know what we do to rapists in here?" I said licking my lips seductively to taunt him.

I knew in my heart that one of us wouldn't make it out of this cell alive, but if it was going to be me, I would be talking my shit. A real man died on his feet not on his knees. Wayne took a deep breath.

"You know what, old man? I have imagined this day for years. I made some plans for you, baby. So, talk all your shit while your mouth still free because the first thing I'm going to do, is shove that fake ass wooden leg so far down your throat, you going to have splinters in your spine!" he said while turning towards Officer Peddle Way so that he could unlock his cuffs. "Remember you told me real men didn't run to the law they handled things themselves? I prayed that God kept you safe all these years, old man so I could handle you myself!" Wayne said to me smiling.

The officer saluted Me and exited the room, shutting the cell door firmly behind him and sealing our fate. No matter who emerged victorious, I knew that two lives would be lost. If Wayne killed Me, he would spend the rest of his life in prison. If I killed Wayne, I wouldn't have consequences besides extra years added to the life sentence I was already serving.

Peddle Way

The last thing I heard was the older man's screams for mercy.

"That one was for you, Netta Boo." I said looking up at the sky and heading to the Warden's office to turn in my badge.

I had already put in my two weeks' notice and prepared for this day. I knew that even with Mason's connections, he would be no match for a man half his age and fueled with a 30 something year vendetta; Wayne wouldn't give up until either himself or Mason was in a pine box.

Like he told me, the world wasn't big enough for him and the man he thought was his father. I prayed that Wayne killed Mason quickly, not only because of the closure he craved for justice for his mother's life, but also so Mason could stop running around the prison filling up the head of younger men to create an *image* of the rehabilitated O.G when in fact he hadn't changed at all; he was still the same nothing ass nigga he had always been.

Chapter Twenty-Eight
<u>Bonnie Bell</u>

*♫ I'm at the borderline of my faith,
I'm at the hinterland of my devotion
In the front line of this battle of mine
But I'm still alive*

*I'm a soldier of love.
Every day and night
I'm a soldier of love
All the days of my life ♫*

"Yes- sir, Colonel sir!" I told my Colonel, as I dropped down to my knees to suck his dick.

I knew if I didn't do it as soon as he commanded, he would go upside my head. I was tired of making up stories about how I fell or accidentally hurt myself and being called the clumsiest Airmen in my group; when truthfully, I was getting my ass kicked by the highest-ranking officer in my Squadron.

At 47, Colonel Richards was old enough to be my father. He was a decorated member of the armed forces, that began his military career at the tender age of 18. With over 20 deployments he was highly respected and adored; everyone wanted to stay on his good side. Which was why I had been doing any and everything to please him since he'd chosen me to be his mistress. He had been married for longer than I was alive and had three sons, with the youngest one being my age. The colonel had a fetish for young women and with new young girls enlisting all the time after graduating high school, he was like a kid in a candy store. He could have his pick of any girl he wanted and if the girl didn't comply, then the officer directly over her would find reasons to give her, her walking papers.

"Yeah, just like that, Bonnie Bell!" he told me calling out my full name as he gripped the back of my long ponytail, shoving his dick down my throat.

He loved to call my full name almost as much as he loved to go upside my head. I could barely visit home because Mama Arlene would start asking questions if I showed up with bruises every time I walked through the door. Plus, he wanted me to be always accessible to him. Whatever girl the colonel chose was his until he was tired of playing with her.

I'd wanted to be in the Air Force since I was 5 years old. Around my high school graduation time, 3 years ago, while all of my classmates scrambled to do college visits and take tests, I didn't apply to college or even take the S.A.T. Instead I continued to study for the ASVAB like I had done since my ninth-grade year. I also continued to participate in R.O.T.C. like I had done for my entire middle and high school career. I didn't need a backup plan, my only desire was to become a pilot in the United States Air Force, travel the world and eventually retire with a fat pension from the military, while continuing to be a pilot for an overpriced airline that would pay me 6 figures for my experience and my expertise.

I did the same thing I always did when the colonel wanted me to perform a nauseating act on him or he wanted to perform an even more nausea inducing act on me; I prayed that he would grow tired of me soon. At the tender age of 22 I really wanted to date and have a boyfriend my age. I didn't want anything serious, just someone to hang out with and post cute social media pictures with like my friends. I wanted to enjoy my 20's and have fun but letting loose would cost me my military career.

I wiped the tears that formed before they could fall. Every time he saw tears it took him longer to cum. I just didn't understand why he chose me out of all the girls he had the option of picking.

"Yeah, just like that. I'm coming. I'm coming you, little whore. Fuck you for making me cheat on my wife, Gloria, because of your big cum catching lips. I want you to swallow my babies like the whore that you are!" he said continuing to degrade me, making me feel like street walking trash. What I didn't understand was, if he wanted a useless whore and somebody to belittle, why didn't he just go and pay a damn prostitute?

Knock. Knock!

"Colonel Richards, are you busy? This is Sergeant Mitchell and Brigadier General Wilson; We need to discuss some serious allegations with you." I heard a man's voice say.

"One-minute, One-minute Sergeant and Brig Gen." the colonel said with his eyes open as wide as saucers.

He looked a little frightened, as he snatched his dick back. So, it took the General to come down there to put some fear into his heart? I prayed that someone had snitched on his old ass. He paced a few steps back and forth and looked at me as if he were contemplating what to do with me, since he only had one way to enter and exit his office. I gathered myself to walk out of the door when he grabbed my arm.

"I wasn't done with you yet!" he said loud enough for only us to hear.

He motioned for me to come to him and I did as I was told. Hiding behind his large desk, careful not to make too much noise, I had never felt as worthless as I did in that moment.

"There have been some allegations, Colonel!" the Sergeant said while clearing his throat uncomfortably.

Even sitting next to a higher-ranking official, who really

had the balls to go up against someone as loved and feared as the Colonel? Me, that's was the fuck who; I was sick of it!

So, I did something I knew I would regret before I had time to talk myself out of it.

Chapter Twenty-Nine
Terri Bell

♫ *You came into my heart*
So tenderly
With a burning love
That stings like a bee

Now that I surrender
So helplessly
You now wanna leave
Ooh, you wanna leave me ♫

"What the fuck do you mean it's just not there for you anymore, D?" I asked my husband completely caught off guard by the words he had just uttered to me.

I turned to my opposite side to face him in our California King-sized bed. Carrying an eight-month stomach full of his son didn't make my turn as quick and graceful as I would have liked. I faced my gorgeous husband of 6 years and my man of 12. He was the father of my 4-year-old daughter, Souvenir, my high school sweetheart, and even though I knew it wasn't right, I loved him more than God, my daughter, my family, all my friends, and anyone else I had ever come in contact with.

Daryl had been my first everything.

The first time I saw the love of my life, I was standing at my locker directly across from the boy's bathroom. Mama Arlene had stayed up with me all night pressing my waist length hair. I had gone down to Walter's in downtown Atlanta and bought me a few pairs of new sneakers; she also took me to Ross to buy a couple new outfits. I was so excited and nervous to be starting high school but as long as I had my best friend, Clara, whom lived next door to us with her mother and stepfather, I knew that I could take on anything.

At 5"6 Clara was taller than me, but all skin and bones. Whenever I wanted to aggravate her, I would call her Tree because of her boyish, curve-less figure. However, her cat like green eyes and light skinned complexion still made all the boys crazy about her. I always envied her for her features and her complexion because even though I wasn't lacking in the body department, but if I had a dollar for every time one of my classmates joked about my dark skin or my wide nose, I would have enough money for a skin bleaching and a nose job.

Daryl was coming out of the boy's bathroom wiping his wet hands on his Girbaud jeans, when I noticed him. His muscular build screamed football player, but he wasn't on our school team. His big lips and deep-set eyes looked odd on his young face but with the eye that I had for all things beautiful, I knew that he would grow into his features and be swoon worthy. I wasn't wrong.

The boys who were looked over in high school usually grew up to be the sexy and successful men. Meanwhile, most of the jocks that we pursued grew up to fat, unemployed, with 5 kids, and living at home on their mother's couch.

Daryl and I had a class together and, I would always admire him from the back of the room. He raised his hand to answer every question, not caring that the other boys would tease him or think he was a nerd.

It was Valentine's Day when I decided to make my move on him. While all the girls were waiting for little red heart invitations, for our high school Valentine's Day dance, I walked up to him and put one in his hand. Clara thought I'd lost my mind, but I didn't care. She didn't see in him what I saw in him.

He had been mine since.

Daryl graduated Valedictorian and put himself through Morehouse College, while working for Taco Bell, which was only a few blocks from the campus. He Majored in Political Science and Government because of his passion for the law. Afterwards, he graduated Summa Cum Laude from Emory University Law School. I decided to take a different route than my man and studied Psychology, while I attended Spellman. After graduating the top of my class, I accepted a counseling position with the State of Georgia with a very competitive salary. A year into my career, while we were vacationing for my birthday in The Bahamas, our first little angel was conceived on the secluded Island of Mayaguana. I knew the moment after we made love that we had conceived our first child; I vowed to name either him or her Souvenir because I couldn't have taken home a better gift.

"Terri Bell, we haven't been happy for months. You put up this façade like we're this perfect family to Mama Arlene, your work friends, Delta sorority sisters, and anybody else that will listen, but this marriage has been over for a long ass time. I cheat on you in your face and you know I do. I purposely leave you with all the bills, leave you all the responsibilities when it comes to our daughter; I disrespect you and talk to you terribly, I don't even touch you! I pity fucked you when you were sad about that promotion you got passed up on, that is how you got pregnant with our son. I hate being with you and every day I am married to you I feel like a caged animal!" he said to me calling me by my maiden name, as casually as if we were discussing the weather.

"Why are you holding on to me? I do all these things so a light bulb will go off in your dumb ass head and you will say hey I'm Terri , I'm gorgeous, smart, I make damn near 6 figures, I have a body that looks like I just jumped off a surgeon's table and I don't have to take shit from an insensitive man that doesn't realize that. Instead, you just put up with it and put up with it. Is the verbal abuse not enough? Do I have to start going upside your damn head like your daddy did your mommy to make you get it?" he asked me with disgust.

I stared in his eyes as tears filled mine. Even though his words were laced with their usual hateful venom, everything he was saying was the God knows truth. It was around our 4th year of marriage that I noticed the change in Daryl. I looked over it because I didn't want to be the woman that gave up on her man. People always said Marriage came in cycles. Sometimes you were crazy about your spouse and sometimes they drove you so crazy, you wanted to take out a policy and murder their ass. I tried to refrain from constantly nagging him; I took over all the household chores and cooking so I wouldn't disturb him with the petty details of the house, even though we both worked the same number of hours every day. I read self-help books, suggested couples' therapy, did individual counseling when he didn't show up for the sessions I paid for, and I looked the other way when he claimed he had late meetings but came home and jumped straight in the shower, and left lip stick stained shirts for me to launder.

I even took on a second job to keep up the lifestyle that we had created. Our big ass house in Douglassville GA, our daughter's private school tuition, the note on my 2019 Mercedes G-Class, and all the bills in the house were paid by me. I knew I deserved better and at this point, I was no longer in love with Daryl. I just didn't want to break up my family and end up alone. I didn't want to be another attitude ridden, neck rolling, submission fearing statistical black girl, that couldn't keep a man, so I put up with his shit.

"Till Death Do Us Part, Daryl!" I told him and turned my back to him in our bed, so he wouldn't see the tears that rolled down the side of my face and onto my satin pillow.

"Well, while you're being married and waiting for Death, I will continue to do the single shit I been doing and embarrass your ass out here until you agree to a divorce. Another one of your sorority sisters slid in my DM's a few hours ago, she said she wants to know what some District Attorney Dick hit like. Who am I to deprive her of that?" he asked me angrily getting out of our bed.

I looked at the poster sized picture of us, framed next to our mounted 65-inch Samsung smart TV, we were attending his first all-black luncheon after he'd been elected Fulton County's District Attorney. I was so proud of my man that day as he rubbed elbows with Atlanta's elite. There were state and federal judges from Atlanta and surrounding counties, Sheriff's and deputies, the chief of police and officers; even the Mayor was in attendance. I sat on a highchair with my legs crossed and sipped a mimosa from across the room, while I watched my man. Rubbing my small, slightly showing baby bump with his daughter inside of me, I began to feel like I'd finally achieved the perfect life I'd always dreamed of. My daydream must have lasted longer than intended because my sweetie startled me when he kissed me gently on my neck to bring me back to reality.

"Take a picture with me beautiful, I'm the luckiest man here." he whispered in my ear as he grabbed my hand gently to ease me onto my feet.

He treated me like I was made of Porcelain since he discovered I was carrying his child; the treatment was multiplied by a thousand when he found out that I was carrying his little princess. He rubbed my ass and leaned closer to whisper in my ear.

"That better just be orange juice in that drink. If you have my baby out here cross eyed like Judge Reynolds, I'm going to kick your ass." I laughed at him putting my head on his shoulder.

Even pregnant my black, spaghetti strapped, slide slit, form fitting, dress could stop traffic. My waist length tresses were side parted, and silk pressed. My makeup was flawless, and my Smokey eyes popped dramatically off my nude lip. There was no need for highlighter, thanks to the natural glow my daughter provided.

"Ok love birds; turn around, I have to get a picture of my favorite couple!" Clara, my best friend, and the assistant district attorney of Dekalb County said as she snapped our picture.

She was dressed to kill in a black satin 2-piece pants suit with no shirt underneath the jacket. I guess when you paid as much as she did for perfect breast, you could ditch a shirt and a bra whenever you felt the need. Gone was the gap-toothed smile she felt insecure about throughout her adolescence. She had gotten her huge sign on bonus and taken it straight to the best dentist in Atlanta. She had also ditched her stick figure for perfect C cups, round hips, and an ass that deserved to be on somebody's pole. However, the only poles she twerked on, were the influential men in the justice system that could further her career.

Her reputation had preceded her, and all the powerful Judges, Clerks, and male attorneys in Georgia had her on speed dial. She thought all the women were envious of her because of her looks and body, but they just wanted to keep from snapping her neck because she couldn't stay away from their husbands. I was the only friend she had left because she had fucked over all the others.

I wondered if my husband was going to meet my hoe ass best friend, because he didn't say a name. I waited until I heard his car pull off and jumped up from the bed grabbing, my cell phone. I opened the app I'd paid for to track his whereabouts and slipped on some black jeans, my black timberlands, and a black hoodie. I went into my dresser and pulled out my 45.

I prayed for my best friend's sake that my husband wasn't on his way to meet her because it would be a shame for her to have gotten all that surgery to only look good in her casket.

Chapter Thirty
Officer Reynolds

When I stepped into the cell following an anonymous tip, I'd never seen such a gruesome scene in my entire life. As one man feasted on the flesh of the other man, like a Hannibal with a crazed expression, I backed out of the cell slowly, while calling over my radio for backup. It was a scene that would eventually make me quit my job at the prison, spend hundreds of dollars, and years in therapy to forget.

TO BE CONTINUED....

WANT TO INTERACT WITH T'ANN MARIE & HER TEAM? JOIN OUR READERS GROUP ON FACEBOOK @ *T'ANN MARIE PRESENTS: THE HOUSE OF URBAN LITERACY*! **WIN PRIZES, BE APART OF LIVE BOOK DISCUSSIONS & MORE!**

T'Ann Marie
PRESENTS

Are you looking for a publishing home that will mold you to become a better writer?

T'Ann Marie Presents, is now accepting submissions in the following genres:

- *Urban Fiction
- *Romance
- *Street Lit
- *Paranormal
- *BWWM
- *Erotica
- *Women's Fiction
- *Christian Fiction

For consideration, please submit the first 3 chapters of your finished manuscript & contact information to:

TAnnMarieSubs@gmail.com

Let us make your dreams, Reality!

Want to join our mailing list?!

Just send your email address by text to:

Text
TMPUPNEXT
to 22828 to get started.

Message and data rates may apply.

Made in the USA
Monee, IL
24 September 2021